inhumanity

Tatenda Charles Munyuki

inhumanity

Tatenda Charles Munyuki

Harp Bookz International

Inhumanity

First published in Zimbabwe in 2014
Harp Bookz International
an imprint of Tatenda Charles Munyuki Publishing

Copyright © Tatenda Charles Munyuki 2014
Cover Illustration Copyright© Straightline Designz 2014
Cover illustration by Straightline Designz 2014

The moral rights of the author have been asserted

ISBN   978 0 7974 6162 8

Printed and bound by Harp Bookz International, Harare, Zimbabwe.
harpbookz@gmail.com

facebook.com/tatendacmunyuki

www.tcmpublishingzim.com

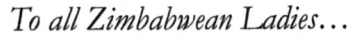

To all Zimbabwean Ladies...

Part One

Ruvimbo

April 2002 – Harare

Chapter 1

Twelve years had passed since independence and two years had gone into the new millennium. It was on the 18th of April 2002.

Ruvimbo wasn't a born free and forgetting wasn't easy for her as the years matured. The air was still filled with post-war grievances and the diversified population was trying to adapt to the alleged *equality*.

Equality existed insofar as all the people paid their taxes, took part in free market competition and, above all, racism was annulled. Her quest in life was to provide *justice* in a world corrupted by daily evil.

Ruvimbo lived in a neighbourhood full of Europeans. Her occupation made her one of the few independent Africans who made a lot of money. Her neighbours were friendly people and in turn, she treated them well.

Being single for Ruvimbo was a necessity rather than a lifestyle. Her mission in life was to leave as few of *them* as possible. Every day was a victory for her. Her *diary's* pages were growing with a list of those she had dealt with already. To her, it was a destiny – who she was and she was proud of it.

Deep inside her, the beast slept only to rise at the most appropriate of times. Her intentions were good toward a higher goal or out of love for the whole.

Tendai stared at her sister for a while. She was a *born-again* person who believed in forgiving sinners. At times, she often wondered if being a toddler at the time her parents had been killed defined her feelings. She had witnessed her parents' murders and she knew what it meant to Ruvimbo. She was constantly concerned about her big sister. Ruvimbo claimed to be a born-again Christian, but had she truly forgiven those who had butchered their parents?

As Ruvimbo slept that day, her mind was on the new *white man* she had met at a dinner party on the previous weekend. His character wasn't important to her, but his status in life and family tree were. Her associates at *Grant and Associates* – the legal firm she worked for – at times teased her calling her a gold digger. She was famous for going out with wealthy white men. If only they knew, she thought, they would thank her for the favour she was doing for her race.

Thinking about him more, Ruvimbo woke up and produced her *secret diary*. It was coated in black and was about eighty pages thick. She took her pen and licked its cap as she counted the names. Her latest find would make him number *twenty-one*. Her face lit up as she fantasized of him and of how he was going to be worthy of her *cause*.

Ruvimbo met her date the following night and took her time to flirt with him. She had one objective and time was of the essence.

'So, Ruvimbo, tell me more about yourself,' her date, Caucasian man in his thirties, asked holding her soft hand.

Ruvimbo looked around and admired her date's choice of hotel. Most of the people in it were white, Indian and rich black people. If only she was interested more in mingling with crowds, she knew she could have enjoyed it.

'On a first date, I usually let the man do the talking,' she said, her eyes on him. He was easy to seduce, she noted.

The *date* gave in and did most of the talking. Ruvimbo played her cards perfectly and as the evening progressed, she knew that she had her man. He was already head over toes over her. His eyes were coloured by an uncontrollable desire as he scanned her. Ruvimbo played to his weakness and they had booked a room by eight o'clock that evening.

Ruvimbo tried to think of what she was doing, but her conscience told her to believe in her overall cause. The purpose of it all overcame the acts. Having done it many times before, she noticed how good she was in bed, manipulating her victim. The lawyer in her knew that what she was doing was unlawful to every extent, not to mention sadistic. The justice in her made her feel as if she was on top of all situations.

Ruvimbo's date was too blinded by lust to think about whom he was dealing with. He spent what he thought to be three of the best hours of his life with Ruvimbo.

As the night warmed up, Ruvimbo lay beside her date sweating from the heightened exchange of passion. The man was busy snoring now, his half-covered body glistening with sweat. Ruvimbo stared at the room's ceiling and watched its fan rotate. She smiled a smile of one who had succeeded. This was officially number twenty-one.

Chapter 2

Francis Domboka was a physician who had experienced the thick and thin during the *Second Chimurenga War*. He was trained by a Russian doctor who had been commissioned to the country as part of a missionary aid group.

When his elder brother's children lost their parents because of the same war, he had used the Russian's influence to take them into his care and it was all because of a man called Jorum.

Jorum K. Westwood had owned a huge farm that was adjacent to the Dombokas' village home. The Dombokas' tribe had survived the land invasion because they were well known for their intelligence when it came to farming and ploughing through droughts. Westwood had seen them as a resourceful crowd just in case the future was to require their use.

Most of the remaining land was given to religious missionaries who were paid to feed the local folks with peaceful psychology to prevent any uprisings. The years came, everybody living in a calm environment.

The first signs of unrest developed when Adam – the first child of the Dombokas – fell in love with one of Westwood's girls. Ruvimbo's brother met the Westwood's girl quite by accident. He used to sneak through the barriers built by Westwood demarcating his land from the rest and help some of Westwood's hard worked labourers on pig and poultry tending skills. Not used to seeing white women, Adam was enchanted by her smooth white skin and flowing blond hair. Genetically gifted with a complexion that was saved from the sunlight by the frequent cloudy and rainy weather in the region, Adam was light skinned enough to catch the eye of the girl. Westwood had barely noticed that Adam wasn't one of his slave-workers for things went well for him to look twice.

The two lovers met secretly for seven months before one of the maids found out and told Mrs Westwood. Afraid of the trouble it would cause if her husband knew she had wisely lectured her daughter and forbade her to see Adam.

Months later, Westwood's farm was scattered with scared black workers. The rumours that somebody amongst them had impregnated the boss's daughter spread around like air. A few knew who the possible father of the unborn child was and some of them fled from the farm in fear of getting involved in what was going to be the scandal of scandals. Nobody was more frightened than Mrs Westwood was. She knew what her husband was capable of.

In the dark, Mr Westwood was happy for her daughter thinking that the baby belonged to one of their neighbours' sons whom they often associated with. The neighbours in question were the other settlers who owned farms that were found next to Westwoods.

A lot of people died the day the stillbirth child was born. Having been given instructions by Mrs Westwood to suffocate the baby to death if it was mixed, the midwife had followed her madam's secret demands. Nobody else knew that the baby was born alive. The mother of the dead child had been unconscious from long labour pains to witness her father's stricken expression. Westwood nearly had a heart attack when he saw what her daughter had produced. He had produced a shotgun and a bag of ammunition. He rounded up all his workers and lined them up. He asked them for the person responsible. The unity of the workers was broken when six of them were shot blank when they failed to give an answer or a satisfying one.

Westwood had left with a lorry and returned with a few of his nasty friends including an armed mob of rebellious locals. They had raided the Dombokas' land and Adam was killed together with two of his brothers and an uncle. Powerless, the Dombokas mourned in silence. The few missionaries who felt saddened by the brutalities had comforted them. Ruvimbo's remaining uncle, Francis, was taken by a Russian missionary to train as a doctor's assistant so that he would later look after the Dombokas with professional skill if ever they were to face another raid and somebody got badly injured.

Westwood lost his daughter after she learned what her mother and midwife had done to her baby. She had stabbed herself with a kitchen knife. Looking for someone to blame, Westwood had accused one of the maids of murdering his beautiful daughter. The household all knew that it was suicide, but had minded their business.

Six years had passed since Adam and his brothers were killed. Drunk the following day after burying his daughter, Westwood ordered one of his loyal workers to shoot the maid. The innocent maid turned out to be one of the Dombokas' daughters who had eloped to work for the Westwoods because she had fallen in love with one of their workers who had taught her how to read a Bible.

Westwood didn't know this until the day his wife, last daughter, including the midwife who had delivered and killed Adam's baby were poisoned to death. The culprit was one of the Dombokas' sons who had discovered that his sister was murdered in cold blood. The Second Chimurenga War had already started and resistances were sited almost everywhere in the country. Westwood was affected so much by the death of his beloved ones that he raided the Dombokas' land again and killed Ruvimbo's parents.

Chapter 3

From a very young age, Ruvimbo's mind was filled with horrifying images of how her parents had been butchered to their deaths. These were memories that had permanently haunted her. The only way she could calm herself without snapping into insanity was fulfilling her *destiny*. She had made peace with her mental condition when she had graduated from college twelve years ago into a gifted legal expert.

Born in a family of eight children, she was the second from last. Of the eight children, they were only three of them remaining. Ruvimbo's older brother Bernard was a civil servant. He was forty years old, had a wife and two boys. He was the only brother left to inherit the Dombokas' name in her family.

To Ruvimbo, Bernard was lost. He had distanced himself from the family and it was six long years since she had heard from him. He hadn't even invited them to his wedding. It was pretty clear that he didn't want anything to do with his sisters and uncle.

Tendai was the last-born and she was twenty-six years old. She lived with their uncle and was currently concluding her postgraduate studies to become a specialised Veterinary Surgeon. Tendai's status in life had solidified the notion that, although the Dombokas were a family stained by a precarious past full of bad fortune, they were a gifted few.

Most of the ideologies Ruvimbo had learnt were mainly European. She had cherished the lecturers because they had taught her quite a lot about imperialism. Her favourite subject was History where she had learnt about *hypocritical Norsemen*. Her main concern was how superpowers manipulated their advantages.

Growing up with British and Russian children had given her the upper hand when it came to being fluent in English. Her fluency had dominated her mother's language and although she could still speak Shona, she sounded more like a British lady. Her accent was one of the attributes that readily attracted men of all races. The other attributes consisted of her flawless beauty. Ruvimbo was tall, had very long black hair, high cheekbones, extremely light-skinned and, above all, had a body that had everything a woman would envy for. Her appearance was her most lethal weapon for almost all men were frequently victim to it.

What not all these men knew were Ruvimbo's beliefs in idealism. She believed that the rightness of actions was wholly determined by the amount of happiness and suffering resulting there from. The needs of the many of her countrymen overweighed the few.

The outburst of many diseases, viruses and plagues in Africa deepened as the years progressed. Many were still suffering from current inflation rates that the millennium had brought. Years of practising law as both a state and – most currently – a private lawyer, didn't soothe her off the bile she felt for the other race. She wished endlessly that the entire Caucasian race would be erased off the face of the Earth. Getting into Law had been a start, but when she had heard of new diseases that were daily becoming a threat to the survival of humanity, she had dreamt more.

When she was in her late teens, Ruvimbo had dreamt of becoming a doctor for a while. She had admired what her uncle was in society, but only she understood what she had in mind. After finishing her studies, it hadn't taken her long to asses her position in the community. She was a beautiful successful young African woman who possessed a British accent. White men craved for her hard and then did she think of a new plan.

Turning twenty-eight in 1995, on her short holiday visit to Mozambique, she unexpectedly met a young man who was a specialist from America who was in the country on a major research on a deadly new virus. The virus was so hard to detect that only a few foreign specialists could spot it before the death of the infected. A virus that took its time in killing and it did so very hideously. Ruvimbo couldn't get the man to tell her the name of the virus, so she called it *Istreblyat'*, a Russian translation of the word *eradication*.

On her birthday's evening, as a single independent woman, she had seduced the CDC worker to show her some of his work and, seeing him in the coming days, had managed to steal an expensive blood storing cooling box where she stored four vials of blood contaminated with the virus. Two weeks later, she lost her *virginity* to a wealthy white man in his late fifties. The man died weeks later from *Istreblyat'*.

Eight years later, Tendai woke her sister and prepared breakfast for her. It was a lovely April's Saturday. Her sister had come in late last night and news that she had won her latest case had made the news on the television broadcast that morning. Ruvimbo was already famous. Tendai always wondered why at thirty-four years old and looking the way she looked, her sister was still single and not searching. The youngest Domboka wanted a taste of family. Her last brother had disowned himself from the family and she wished that one day he would change his mind. She yearned to know her cousins and their mother too. Her uncle and his family were a lovely lot, a family of Christians who helped as many people as they could.

Ruvimbo was her role model and the loving sister she thanked God for giving her. Tendai had never seen her sister going out with a man who wasn't white. It mystified her when she thought of how Ruvimbo reacted when it came to sensitive issues involving the two most famous races in the world.

The young sister thought that Ruvimbo was perhaps trying to bond with them, to understand them more in order to forget what the past held. Life was short to live holding grievances against each other. Forgiving others was as easy as not forgiving. What was needed for one to forget, Tendai knew, was to overlook the sin and accept the actions of the sinner.

Ruvimbo knew just how religious her little sister was. Tendai didn't know much about *life*. Life consisted of people and everyone served a particular purpose in it. Ruvimbo also believed that people, who had had very little experience with the suffering of others and, especially the suffering of young people and children, were sometimes incapable of experiencing the kind of feelings she was having.

Her purpose in life was to wipe out the white race, not because one of them had murdered her family, but because the white race was a flawed kind. She had to infect *every one of them* with *Istreblyat'* so they would all would die, even the unborn children. After breakfast, Ruvimbo read from her diary and was pleased with her progress. To date, she didn't show signs of having any dark secret and looked as healthy as any normal human. The fact that she had seen many crumble from *Istreblyat'* and her having it stored safely at her house without catching it made her believe more that she was destined to live long till her mission was over. She knew that she didn't have much time to live a legacy for anytime was *death time*, but she also knew that she had to infect as many white men as she could with the deadly disease.

White men were like another kind of virus that needed eradication to her. Many people had lost their lives because of the war. Ruvimbo gazed at her diary once more and smiled. The names of her victims were neatly written in black ink.

The names all had one thing in common. They had a single family name, *Westwood*. During her university days and after, she had searched for the man who had ordered the killing of her parents. It took her five years to gather up enough information on the man and his descendants.

The Westwoods had killed Adam's son, her brothers and sister, so their sons and daughters were also going to pay. She had endured the psychological unrest of having the images of her parents being killed slowly and painfully in her head and so were the Westwoods going to die slowly and painfully. It was a vendetta she had dedicated her life to.

'I thought you were coming with me to see uncle today,' Tendai said as Ruvimbo parked her car that afternoon.

'Something came up,' Ruvimbo replied, brushing her hair from her face. 'I'm meeting with a big client.'

'For business or for pleasure?'

Ruvimbo grinned at her. 'Probably both – he is looking for a new lawyer to represent his trading enterprise.'

'So it's a he, why am I surprised?' Tendai smiled.

She stared out of the windshield and saw three kids playing on the lawn. The neighbourhood was in Mount Pleasant, a peaceful one in which her uncle had lived for seven years. The houses found there were pretty expensive for the average citizen earning a good salary.

'I'll pass by towards the evening. Please tell uncle that I'll see him then,' Ruvimbo said as her sister made her way out of the car.

An hour later, she drove through the gates of a huge house that was decorated by many palm trees. Her new client was a wealthy white man who had inherited a lot of money from a family business that had managed to survive through the war and after it. The house's lawns were immaculate, tended by a few African workers. As she parked her car in the driveway, a bulky lady wearing a white suit greeted her cheerfully. Her face turned pink at the cheeks, as she looked her up and down. It was evident that the woman was taken aback by Ruvimbo's beauty.

'It's hard to come across anyone of your kind who looks like you do, dear,' the woman smiled taking her hand.

'Anyone of my kind?' Ruvimbo re-checked.

'Yes, dear, I have had a fair share of black girls who didn't have fine long hair – is it real – and whose skin wasn't the imitation of burnt charcoal.'

Ruvimbo stared at the lady, stunned at her openness. She felt deeply insulted and created some space between them.

They entered the house, which was a magnificence of its own making. It had a staircase that curled upwards to the first floor. Pictures of the family were hung all over what appeared to be the foyer of the house.

'A beauty, isn't it?'

'Huh?' Ruvimbo woke up from her trance of admiring the house's interior designs. 'Oh, yes, it is beautiful.'

'My husband built the house in the 80s after he sold the goldmine near Shamva. My son inherited it, of course, when he died in 95 after a short illness,' the lady said, leading her to what looked like a dining room.

A man wearing a black suit was sitting on one of the sofas with a newspaper in his grasp. He looked up to see the two come in and carefully folded the paper. He smiled at the visitor and rose to offer his hand.

'Ms Domboka, it's nice for Mr Grant to finally send you,' the man said in a voice that was filled with both charm and respect. They shook hands. 'I am Paul Westwood. I believe you have already acquainted with my talkative mother, Diana.'

'Oh, Paul, treating people with courtesy isn't being what you call talkative,' Mrs Westwood said. 'Mollie on the other hand is talkative. No wonder my grandchildren are getting deaf from all her shouting.'

Paul persuaded his mother to leave them in peace after a while. He offered Ruvimbo a seat and sat after her.

'I am so sorry you had to experience that, Ms Domboka. Mollie and I tend to ignore her mumbling a lot that she takes it all up on our visitors.'

Ruvimbo smiled at him. 'She has the mouth of a solicitor, I understand, Mr Westwood. She speaks her mind and that is good,' she said.

'That's a first,' Paul said surprised. 'Most of our friends say she is very nosey to start with. Mollie and she don't see eye to eye.'

'Mollie?' Ruvimbo was curious.

'Er – sorry, Mollie would be my wife. She is out for the day with our two boys at some birthday party. Do you care for something to drink?'

'Water would be okay, please.'

'Sure,' Paul rose and left the room to return a minute later with a tray that had a crystal bottle of cold water accompanied by a glass. He poured some water into the glass and handed it over to Ruvimbo.

Ruvimbo drank slowly, studying Paul secretly. He was the first really handsome Westwood she had come across. He had dark eyebrows, his hair so black that it was almost shiny. His face was warm and attractive, but his eyes showed that he had a lot to hide. Ruvimbo had experience as a lawyer to notice what many would overlook when they looked at this disarming man.

'Can we begin?' Paul said clearing his throat.

He was aware of the glances Ruvimbo threw at him. He had married a very beautiful wife, the daughter of a baron, but this intelligent looking lawyer was like a dream to him. He tried not to stare.

'As you wish, Mr Westwood,' Ruvimbo replied.

'Please call me Paul.'

'Mollie would appreciate I call you Mr Westwood, sir,' Ruvimbo replied casually.

Paul blushed and shrugged into a comfortable position. 'As you wish, Ms Domboka,' he grinned.

Ruvimbo smiled back and let her eyes do the trick. 'What do you want Grant and Associates to do for you?'

The rest of the conversation was business, but Paul was left confused. He had a lot of knowhow with women both white and black. The problem was that he didn't know if Ms Domboka was giving him mixed signals. He knew though that he had to be very careful. His next project required a very organized well up woman.

The project was gender specific, and for it to excel, it needed an African woman and who could be more perfect than a very successful beautiful lawyer who, to flavour things up, had a British accent?

Ruvimbo arrived at her uncle's house in the afternoon and found him sitting on the front porch in an argument with his wife and niece. She guessed long before she had reached them that it was about politics.

Francis Domboka was to some extent a war veteran who believed that political parties were essential for the growth and balance of power in a nation. His wife and Tendai were anti-that policy claiming that parties or no parties, the growth and balance of power in a country was determined by how educated and God fearing the people of that country were. A debate usually took hours to be carried on whenever something came up from the media. Francis was a doctor with war experience, but he didn't boast about it. He always took in the views of the others, but never derailed from his points and facts. The white settlers had made life a living hell for him and his family, but being a doctor had taught him the value of life.

As they had dinner that evening, Tendai introduced a topic on *death sentences* including the life in prison sentence. The debate was slow to heat up and when the younger children left the room for sleep, the words increased.

'Human life has value, not price. It is worth not cost, my niece. You people of the earthly Law tend to forget that,' Dr Domboka said.

Ruvimbo grunted and put her feet on the sofa where Mrs Domboka was busy braiding Tendai's long hair. They were relaxing in the sitting room where a huge TV set occupied the centre of an expensive entertainment system. Nobody took interest in what it was showing.

'Uncle, you must be aware of human ethics. They are all so simple to understand,' Ruvimbo said. Her uncle was a smart man and debating with him wasn't simple. 'The rightness of an action is wholly determined by the amount of happiness and suffering resulting therefrom.'

'You are right, my dear, but happiness and suffering aren't addictive. No one man deserves to die so that the others can be happy. Will it be better off killing sick, old people in the interest of the higher development of the race or people?'

Ruvimbo grinned and gave her sister a knowing look. 'We are talking about killing criminals who kill innocent people to prevent more killings and guard people from more unhappiness. It is so necessary, so useful.'

'You mean to say these death sentences are meant to do the

community a favour by exterminating these criminals?' Dr Domboka said. 'Where is the love of civilization there, Ruvimbo? If we kill the culprit, what makes us any different from the culprit?'

'What you are referring to, uncle, is a world that is filled with nothing, but love where we don't have criminals to kill because of their crimes. There's no such world. Nobody can love everyone to forgive them of exterminating sins.'

Tendai witnessed the strain on her sister's face and knew that forgiveness was something she had never had in her. 'If we learn to forgive others, the Bible says we'll also learn to love everyone unconditionally,' she contributed to the debate.

Ruvimbo shook her head in disagreement. *You have a lot to learn, dear sister,* she thought. 'It isn't possible for any living human being – even the moral or most noble person – to love all mankind. It's self-deceiving and hypocritical to believe and claim that one can possibly love all mankind.'

'Human relationships are bad omens,' Dr Domboka laughed nervously. He knew that what his niece had said was nothing, but the very truth of the human race.

Chapter 4

The goal to all human activity is living, the ability to survive. To Ruvimbo, the Caucasian race had no right to existence. The daily news was replete of Boers' nasty atrocities down South and many countries in the Middle East were crying foul about the Americans.

Same pigmentation, same minds lead to the same fate, Ruvimbo thought. She was very proud of being able to serve her race and many others by doing something. She was on the verge of vaporizing the Westwoods' family tree. There was only one vital branch left to trim and she believed that her *right to existence* was close to being accomplished on many levels.

Ruvimbo's desire for living was rooted in the desire to make the world a better place. She didn't fear death for she knew that the future had nothing new to offer for her if she didn't first finish what she had started. She was not thinly veiled by boredom, but her energy to annihilate the Westwoods was stronger than any drug.

Grant and Associates were very happy to offer her as their representative to Westwood Company's innovation called *Women of Tomorrow.* An organization that was going to be led by a female CEO who was going to guide it to the brims of entirely new ventures never seen before in Zimbabwe. *WT* was going to be supported by *Heaven's Ministry,* an excessively influential church that Paul had started in 1987. WT was to be well known for its charitable work in rural areas where it offered to rebuild houses, electrifying them and create cattle dipping sites for the village residents.

Paul had offered the CEO position of WT to Ruvimbo. Ruvimbo accepted the offer knowing that she was probably going to leave her firm because of her new occupation. Mr Grant was very happy to see her progress to a higher exclusive position in her career. The lady was full of promise and he envisioned Ruvimbo becoming one of the first most successful African women in Zimbabwe. Her future was very bright.

Ruvimbo met Paul Westwood and Mr Gant to sign her new contract as the CEO of Women of Tomorrow that following week. Her colleagues were saddened to see her go. She had been the anchor of their legal force and losing her was going to leave a crack in the base.

The new and first CEO of WT was happy to leave the firm knowing that this was a step further towards her desires. Her new occupation was going to come with a very healthy package of wealth, which meant that Tendai was going to live a very sound life once she inherited all of *her* things.

Heaven's Ministry drove Women of Tomorrow in its charitable works. The more Ruvimbo was involved with her work, the more she met Paul Westwood and knew about his life.

Paul was an aggressive executive who got what he wanted when he wanted it. He was a devoted Christian who attended every church service held by his church. Ruvimbo had attended two sermons and that's when she had met Molline Grant-Westwood. She was a very lovely lady who was warm and kind. She was British and Ruvimbo later discovered that she was Mr Grant's cousin sister. Her two boys looked more like miniature Pauls with their short well-kept black hair. They had all been born in the country and their dark tanned skin colour showed that they had accustomed to the African sun well.

Going to every major function that Heaven's Ministry held was compulsory for Ruvimbo and she started noticing things she wished she hadn't opened her eyes to. Corruption was everywhere.

'It's a corrupt system, Mrs Westwood,' Ruvimbo argued one day when she had a meeting with Paul and Mollie who were the owners of WT.

She didn't care much about the organization, but people were starting to talk a lot and she didn't want to associate her innocent uncle and family in the chaos. Everyone in the country now knew her as a flashy biased bloodsucking Domboka because of a few things WT and Heaven's Ministry appeared in the papers being accused of.

'There is corruption everywhere – mainly in typical surroundings. It is a cancer at the heart of most third world states, Ms Domboka. We can't do anything about it that hasn't been done already,' Mollie replied frowning.

She didn't really like Ruvimbo very much mainly because of her exquisite beauty. Her husband had wandering eyes and to her, Ruvimbo meant bad news.

'This isn't normal corruption,' Ruvimbo liked the challenge. The lady was her boss, but she did little to scare her. 'This is widespread corruption, Mr and Mrs Westwood. It's creating a climate of mortal degeneration and making a mockery of our efforts to those we are trying to help.'

'This is business, Ms Domboka. In business, there is always widespread corruption – especially if it is as profitable as ours is becoming. Tell her, Paul!' Mrs Westwood junior said firmly.

Paul just nodded, his expression focused like someone who was weighing the points of the argument to see which side was right to back and which was lethal no to.

'In the long run, this will divert the social reform and ethics of those we lead. I know what I'm talking about when I say this will pervert and hamstring development. It will cost us more than what we'll gain in the future like a badly planned court case.'

Mrs Westwood junior frowned and folded her arms 'We all know that you are a very talented and successful lawyer, Ms Domboka, but corruption is seldom a court matter however widespread it maybe in the society. Honey – let's leave this hot place and go and see my dentist as we planned.'

Paul and Mollie left Ruvimbo fuming. She had no call in many things in WT so there was nothing she could do. The majority of the high-ranked employees of the organization were white, Indian or French. She later discovered her position as the CEO was just a strategy to make the company popular and receptive to the local population. She hated these white people for taking advantage of the innocent people who had joined WT with the hope of a fresh start being led by one of their own, her.

Ruvimbo estimated that she couldn't do anything about the ever-rising corruption that was painting WT. Mollie was no lawyer, but she was dead on right. Corruption was often condemned as a deviation from the norms of public morality, but the norms were ambiguous. In practice, she had learned that it was difficult to draw a line between expected behaviour and corrupt behaviour.

Ruvimbo saw less of Paul for the rest of the month for he was out of the country. Dealing with his wife was a bore for she had a habit of changing colours like a chameleon.

Mollie chose to be nice when they weren't discussing business, but she was a menace when it came to the policies of the company. It took Ruvimbo another month to realize why. WT was rumoured to be the brainchild of Mollie and as her husband ran many successful businesses in the SADC region, she had thought she needed to be something else than a housewife who was only good at preparing good socializing gatherings. Mollie wanted her husband's respect businesswise. The notion became clearer when Paul's interest in WT waned as the months passed. He didn't care if it was profitable or not and he appeared more interested in Heaven's Ministry than his wife's development.

'Where is Mr Westwood today?' Ruvimbo asked one day as WT officially opened a clinic in Karoi. This was the third time Paul was missing from a major event.

'He took his mother to see someone in Kwekwe,' Mollie replied in a hurt voice.

'He went to see Frank, didn't he?' Ruvimbo said absentmindedly.

Mollie stared at her stunned. 'You know Frank?'

Ruvimbo nodded. 'He told me he had a cousin brother called Frank living in Kwekwe,' she lied without a shade of hesitancy.

'Frank is terribly sick from some new illness, Paul said,' Mollie told her. 'From the way they are saying it, I don't think he will be with us long.'

'Your mother-in-law had to go too?'

'Frank and Paul are...' Mollie stuttered. 'The only Westwoods left in their generation. The past few years has taken away about fifty Westwood, sons and daughters. They have some kind of genetic flaw, I think. I am so scared for my sons.'

Ruvimbo fought down the remorse she felt. Hearing that number from someone else was odd to her. She knew she had to be very careful from now, because the number was huge and suspicious.

It was August when Ruvimbo had her hunches confirmed as correct. Paul wasn't a faithful husband. He liked his eggs with a different flavour. He was more attracted to black ladies who possessed sexual alluring features and since there weren't that many ladies having those features whilst at the same time being white, he settled for light-skinned Africans or coloured women.

Paul's appetite for women disgusted his wife and Ruvimbo was more than aware of it. Her role model as the supporting loving wife was wasted on an egocentric human being. Ruvimbo felt slightly sorry for her having married a Westwood. She was also sorry that a day would come when Mollie was going to suffer the consequences of having the Westwoods' name on her.

'Do you ever think of settling down, Rue?' Mollie said getting ready to leave for a church sermon that was being held at a new church Heaven's Ministry had just opened in Victoria Falls. The two women were guests at a hotel and Ruvimbo was helping her boss get ready.

'Sometimes – I do,' Ruvimbo zipped Mollie's dress for her on the back.

'Men are parasites, they feed up on all your love and after they don't like the taste anymore, they leave you for someone else,' Mollie said.

'Are you having problems with Mr Westwood, again?' Ruvimbo

was patient. This wasn't the first – and possibly not the last – time Mollie confided in her. She had a good ear. 'What's the matter, Mollie?' She pressed gently. Although rivals at times, the two women had moved on to the first name calling stage in their fragile relationship.

'I'm quite mushy about Paul. He treats me like filth,' Mollie complained. She felt old and unwanted. Ruvimbo's graceful self-confident air intimidated her sometimes.

'I'm certain that a day will come when he suddenly realizes what he is missing,' Ruvimbo gave her a friendly smile.

Feeling better, Mollie and Ruvimbo left the hotel to a long tiring service that enhanced the number of parishioners as the presence of Mrs Westwood junior accompanied by Ms Domboka did most of the talking.

The ladies spent the rest of the day going to places of interest. They visited many of the holiday attraction zones around Victoria Falls and Mollie didn't want to leave the place till the following day.

They were scheduled to take the nine A.M. flight to Harare that Monday when the taxi they were in was involved in a tragic accident. Mollie was killed and the driver was badly injured. Ruvimbo was lucky to come out of the accident with a fractured arm and a few cuts and bruises.

Mollie's funeral was held in England in the lands of Wycombe where her ancestors were buried. Paul spent a month consoling his in-laws before he returned home.

Chapter 5

By the summer of 2002, WT had grown into a big organization, which women of all races and all backgrounds had joined. Mollie's sudden death had ironically given the group more meaning and increased its value.

WT was now the main face behind the current new activist rights for women in the country. Women demanded more respect from the male-dominated environment. Many men saw WT as a threat to the well-being of the nation. Women demanding for more freedom at home, more places in the industry and executive ranks in companies, encompassed daily activists. The government's structure was also threatened by this new development.

Paul Westwood soon witnessed the change and how priceless WT was becoming. He put more effort in the company and recruited a few black women to tend executive roles in the organization.

His house was utterly lonely as he walked into the sitting room. He telephoned Ruvimbo just to hear the sound of her voice. He sounded alert. It was early four in the morning on a promising Sunday.

'What's wrong, Mr Westwood?' she asked him.

Paul moaned into the mouthpiece. 'You sound weird, Ms Domboka.'

'I guess I'm tired from the party,' Ruvimbo said.

'I'll see you at church then?'

'I suppose so. Good morning, Mr Westwood,' Ruvimbo hung up.

There was no point in talking to this man at four in the morning. Mollie's death had done a lot. It had showed Ruvimbo the other side of Paul Westwood. Unable to return to sleep, Ruvimbo thought of him wondering if there was a single bone of humanity in the Westwoods' family. Diana didn't act aggrieved by the death of her daughter-in-law. Everyone knew that the two hadn't seen each other eye to eye, but they had at least thought the lady would show signs of compassion or something like that.

Diana was a very direct person. The only thing she praised her memory of Mollie was the organization Mollie had formed. Women of Tomorrow was an achievement and Diana had taken over Mollie's spot in the company as co-owner.

Ruvimbo had to give Diana credit because once a corrupt company was now a meaningful one. She had the blood of a tiger and the wit of a beaver. Many corrupt individuals at WT lost their jobs because of her care-not attitude. She lashed out to anyone who was against her policies. The most important and overlooked element of her efficiency was that she was a feminist. With her position as the CEO of WT put to more use by being given the free reign to exercise her powers, Ruvimbo grew to like the woman. She despised the white race, but Diana's open character made her understand the race more. Diana wasn't a pretender. If she didn't like something, she told you so.

The other thing Ruvimbo admired about the lady was Diana's view towards religion. Paul was convinced that his mother was a hypocrite. She attended all church services and she had a thing or two to say against religion. Members of Heaven's Ministry didn't like her, but had to tolerate her existence, as she was after all the mother of their leader.

'Did you really need to build a church, dear?' Diana said on that Sunday's afternoon as they entertained Ruvimbo and Tendai for lunch. It was probably the hundredth time she had asked this question.

Tendai was very enthusiastic about the meeting. She was however still confused as to why her uncle didn't like the idea that Ruvimbo worked for the family when it was the main reason why she had risen to being one of the most influential women in the land.

'Mother, do we really need to have this conversation – again?' Paul was embarrassed. He didn't like it when his mother picked on his ideas.

'Do you know what I think about the many of you natives who join churches, Tendai?' Mrs Westwood said to her guest. She liked Tendai for she was very attractive like her sister, not to mention that she was a vet. 'I think most of it is for show. We all know that you blacks are traditionally inclined to your voodoo and stuff.'

Tendai gulped on the juice drink she was having. Ruvimbo had pre-warned her of Diana's attitude, but she hadn't warned her that the lady had the air of a revolutionist.

'Uhhhm – I don't know,' she snapped. She smiled to counteract it.

Paul's face fell. 'Mother, can we talk about something else, please.'

'Oh, alright,' Diana said. 'You are very naïve, aren't you, dear? Ruvimbo, do you think men will always have the desire for organized religion?'

Ruvimbo didn't know how to react. She knew that once Diana started there was no stopping her. 'I think not – knowing that that opinion is based on a superficial study of the religious psychology of human beings.'

'Now that's what I am talking about,' Diana celebrated her success with a whooping sound.

'Religion, Mrs Westwood, makes people more civilized and mostly intelligent,' Tendai said.

'I agree, religion is needed for all of us to be organized,' Paul supported her. 'It all has to do with having faith, mother, something I don't think you have.'

Diana smiled ironically and wiped her mouth with a towel. She threw it on her empty plate ready for battle. 'People never cling to their faith simply for what it claims. These so-called intelligent and civilized people of yours defend their religion because it's nothing other than defiance of the majority view.'

'And what is the majority's view?' Tendai asked.

'The one that claims that religion is in fact many ways a highly dangerous replacement of morals.' Diana said and smiled. 'I know Ruvimbo would side me on this one,' she added.

Ruvimbo gazed at them. She was busy separating herself from the debate. Siding anyone would lead to a longer argument and she didn't want to spend the rest of the day at the Westwoods'. The sudden appearance of the maid informing Diana that she had a visitor saved her from giving her point of view.

Frank died on the 3rd of October and the family told the externals that he had suffered from long-term liver cancer. Nobody really knew the truth. Some close members thought he had suffered from AIDS and were afraid of tainting the family's name. Frank was survived by a wife who looked to be sick as well. Her illness showed that she wasn't going to last long and was in the path of following her husband.

Ruvimbo assessed the situation and saw three male Westwoods left in the country. Her extensive research had paid off, it was definite that apart from Paul, and his sons, no one male with the name Westwood remained. Her status at WT had given her adequate resources to further her secret search and do it wide and easily without paying a cent for it than before.

Ruvimbo knew that she could have finished the job already for she had a full vial of *Istreblyat'* left, but she now had other plans. If Paul was to die anytime soon, the Westwood Company was going to crumble because there was no one left to inherit the line. Diana wasn't a capable businesswoman to run the whole company by herself. A strong male figure was needed. The collapse of Paul would mean the collapse of the company and eventually the collapse of WT.

Many women had been empowered for the past few months than in years because of WT. If all that were suddenly to stop, the whole point behind the idea of WT and its meaning would be jeopardized to the level where reform was going to be for nothing. Ruvimbo saw herself as a social ethicist whose works were to be continued, moving towards that ethical goal of empowering black women. She now had two goals to achieve. Making sure that WT was to become an entity of its own became her main goal. Taking care of the last Westwoods was the other.

Days passed as she thought of that perfect plan to hit the two birds with one stone. Her attention was borrowed when her little sister graduated again. It was one of those few happy moments in her life. Tendai became the second doctor to be qualified as a surgeon in the Dombokas' family and Ruvimbo produced tears of pride when she saw how overjoyed her uncle was. The last third generation Domboka graduating to be a doctor had been one of the best things to ever happen to him four years ago. Her becoming a specialised surgeon as well only made him prouder.

'I think I saw Bernard in the crowd,' Tendai told Ruvimbo excitedly.

The two were accompanied by Mrs Domboka in the hall where freshly excited graduates and their families exchanged pleasantries as they tucked into the snacks prepared by the university.

'You saw who?' Ruvimbo was stunned.

'Brother Bernard,' Tendai said, excitedly returning a wave to one of her prior college mates. They weren't that many female veterinary surgeons or even male ones in the country at that level of qualification. It was a proud moment.

Ruvimbo was taken aback. *What was their self-disowned brother doing at the ceremony?* Bernard had made it clear that he didn't want anything to do with the family. Tendai didn't know the real reason why, but her sister did. Ruvimbo knew that by distancing himself from the family he had remaining, Bernard thought he could forget the terrors the Dombokas had faced during the war.

'Why would your brother be here?' Mrs Domboka was just as surprised.

'For quite a number of things that don't concern us,' Ruvimbo said. She despised weak people who ran away from their problems.

'I'd like to see him,' Tendai said.

Ruvimbo was appalled. 'See who – that loser?'

'He isn't a loser,' the ever-forgiving Tendai said.

'What's your definition of a loser?' Ruvimbo was getting impatient.

'I think he came to see us – finally,' Tendai ignored her.

Ruvimbo shrugged. 'Don't confuse fact and fantasy.'

Tendai frowned back, but said nothing. She did want to see the brother she hadn't grown knowing.

The ladies discussed of how well the ceremony was as they made way from the gathering. They came across Dr Domboka having a heated one on one with someone who looked familiar.

Ruvimbo couldn't believe the other man's nerve. 'What are you doing here?' she demanded, forcefully snatching her brother's arm.

Bernard tried to smile and was intimidated by how beautiful his sister had become. He had been following her successful era all these years, but hadn't mastered the courage to face her. He was forever confused of why of all things Ruvimbo had chosen to work for Westwood after all the bad history they had.

His gaze strayed at her side and focused on Tendai. The two girls had done well for themselves in life and he knew that if he hadn't been so proud years ago, he would have become like them. However, that wasn't to be for he had spat on his uncle's face when he was offered help. Bernard blamed Francis for associating with the race that had murdered his family.

'He says he is here to make peace,' his uncle replied for him with a scowl.

'Why now, after all these years?' Ruvimbo said apprehensively.

An attractive lady wearing a pink dress came over and stared. Ruvimbo immediately guessed that this was Bernard's wife. She looked polite and associative, but in her eyes, she appeared like a serpent.

'Meet my wife, Rudo,' Bernard introduced her to the family. Rudo smiled politely at them.

'Why should we want to talk or even see you again, Bernard?' Uncle Francis wasn't going to overlook his nephew's wool-gathering.

It was very hard forgiving someone who had abandoned you when it could have been avoided. Bernard's knife edge-like words were still etched in his memory. His nephew had called him a *traitor*, a Judas who deserved nothing, but to be hanged.

'If you don't want me here, I'm gone!' Bernard said, impatience getting the best of him.

'Please don't –' Tendai tried to make peace.

'Go – damn it, we don't want you!' Ruvimbo cried back. A few people stared in their direction and curiously looked away. 'Just because you see how well everybody has done, you suddenly want to be part of it? What a pathetic little man you are.'

Bernard left with his wife and Tendai was near tears. A good day was ending badly, Ruvimbo thought, but how could she just take him back into her life when Bernard had made it perfectly clear that he wanted no part of it? To her, he was a forsaken misguided pessimist. She was doing her family name a favour and what was Bernard doing except timidly shying off his responsibility?

'Please calm down, *muzukuru*,' Mrs Domboka put a hand on her shoulder.

All agreed that it was very unorthodox to appear at the graduation ceremony without warning them. Bernard hadn't thought that far otherwise he would have done as expected of him, staying away.

Chapter 6

The day Ruvimbo finally made her move on Paul was the day Women of Tomorrow became an independent organization. It was early November and the summer rains had just started falling. The process was quite difficult than Ruvimbo had anticipated, but she had finally got there.

Paul didn't want WT to be an entity of its own – free from the control of Westwood Company and Heaven's Ministry. The organization brought foreign investors to back Heaven's Ministry and the family business as a whole. His mother was however very persistent about the issue. She felt that WT needed to stand by itself, free from a male dominated entity.

Ruvimbo had first won the trust of Mrs Westwood to get her to buy into the idea. She had carefully manipulated the old woman's motives to fit her plans. Mrs Westwood wanted to leave a legacy, something to be remembered by. Her daughter-in-law had given her that opportunity when she had convinced her son to form WT and died leaving it all up to her.

Westwood Company was to sell its shares to Mrs Westwood and Ruvimbo – Diana having 60%, Ruvimbo 30%, whilst the rest were for Heaven's Ministry. When the idea had surfaced, Paul was very reluctant to give in to his mother's wishes. His mother was the last person he wanted to own WT. In the end, Mrs Westwood had offered to exchange all her stake in the Westwood Company for the ownership of WT.

'You are sure you want to give me all those shares?' Paul was awed by his mother's sudden decision.

'I'll never live long to run the business, Paul. I might as well have something of my own before I die,' Diana said.

Her blood pressure had always been a scare a times. She had married Westwood for both the wealth and fame that was accompanied by her upgrade in social identity. This was the final piece to her success.

'I don't know,' Paul said, not convinced.

Diana had always been hands on the family company's assets after his father's death. He was curious at her sudden change of heart.

'If you don't know soon, I promise you I'll sell those shares to someone else,' Diana threatened.

Paul had known his mother wasn't messing around. The shares his mother had were many to make a perky outsider have the power to overtake ownership of Westwood Company. He had concurred to the offer.

'You are what?' Ruvimbo was stunned. She scrutinized Tendai and saw that she wasn't joking.

'Kuda and I've been seeing each other for five years now, Ruvimbo. I love him very much and I agreed to marry him because I want to,' Tendai explained. Ruvimbo was the last person in the family she was telling about Kuda's proposal and her acceptance.

'I don't know this boy.'

Tendai went over to sit on a chair that faced the window of her sister's office. WT's headquarters had exceptional and immaculate offices in a suburb near the CBD. 'He is twenty nine – he isn't a boy anymore,' she said.

'And still, the point is that I don't know him,' Ruvimbo said closing a file she had been working on before Tendai had arrived in with the unsettling news.

'You'll know him soon,' Tendai laughed lightly. 'He wants to meet you very much. He says he has never met a real celebrity.'

Ruvimbo shrugged. 'I'm not a celebrity,' she mumbled.

She knew how empty those words sounded. She was the role

model for many modern day African women. She wasn't yet used to it all for it had occurred in a short space of time.

'Do I receive your blessing then?' Tendai asked hopefully.

'As if my blessing would bless anything,' Ruvimbo said sarcastically.

Tendai shot a look at her. 'Why can't you be happy for me?' she said hurt.

'Forgive me when I can't act jubilant when my little sister comes to my office and suddenly tells me that she is going to get married to someone she has been seeing for five years – someone she never bothered to tell me about or introduce me to,' Ruvimbo fumed. 'Does Uncle Francis know about this?'

'Yes, he does. He has met Kuda quite a number of times now. He approved my decision and agreed to accept the *lobola* in place of our deceased father.'

'Please leave my office, now!' Ruvimbo snapped, pointing at the door.

Tendai looked at her astonished. She was too shocked to notice that Ruvimbo was near tears. They had grown up together and not a single moment had Ruvimbo raised her voice at her. She knew that she was wrong not having told Ruvimbo about Kuda, but every time she had had the chance, she had been so afraid that Ruvimbo wouldn't approve her having a relationship with someone whilst still in uni.

Ruvimbo watched her little sister leave and burst into tears. *What was going on? Why had Tendai kept her in the dark for so long? Wasn't she the good sister everyone claimed she was? If Tendai didn't trust her enough to show her her-to-be husband, then truly what was the point in living anymore?*

That evening, she called Paul and made dinner reservations at a hotel. It was time to implement the final stages of her plan. At the hotel, Ruvimbo shared a suite with Paul. She seduced him and Paul was wise enough to use a condom for the first night. The deaths of his relatives had taught him that negligence of the deadly virus that was circulating out there was a fool's act. He had tested HIV negative at his first go and from experience, he knew that playing it safe was better than anything was.

'Do you think I have AIDS, love?' Ruvimbo flirted with him the second time they had sex.

She had planned to sleep with him a few times to have him hooked before she was to drug him unconscious and inject him with *Istreblyat'* like she had done with all the other Westwood men she had killed.

Paul blushed. 'It's not that, Ruvimbo,' he smiled toying with her hair. 'Perhaps I'm the one who has got it. You know my history.'

They spent the night exchanging passionate love. Paul was on top of the world as all his desires for Ruvimbo were finally satisfied. He had waited too long and the wait had been worth it.

When Diana told her that she had cancer, Ruvimbo was confused. The huge lady had seemed so indestructible. Diana's form began to deteriorate late November and only then did Ruvimbo believe that the old lady was dying slowly and courageously. The cancer had gone far along to be treated. Paul seemed unconcerned about his mother's health, Ruvimbo saw. He mocked her daily and appeared cruel at times. Diana was however a tough lady. She fought her condition with little success, but she was coping with life step by step.

'I'll not be treated like an effigy, Paul,' Diana snapped one day when Paul offered to drive her to the doctor for her check-up.

'Suit yourself, mother. You can drive yourself,' Paul said giving up. 'Harare is after all not London.'

'You can't wait to get rid of me, can't you, son?'

Paul grinned. 'I'll be running WT again, that will be more dinner on my plate.'

Diana eyed her. 'Business comes first to you. Your sod cheeky father taught you well,' she said angrily.

'Just as your mother came first when you went to England and spent three years there leaving me with father – what did you expect?'

Diana looked down. 'Your grandmother was sick. I had to look after her.'

'Just an excuse, mother, it's just an excuse. You could have easily taken me with you, but you chose to leave me behind.'

'You should be very careful, Paul, your children might grow up to become a prick just like you,' Diana warned.

'I learned from the Masters, remember? Having parents like you has been a big lesson in my life.'

'I'm your mother for Christ's sake, Paul. I know you better than you know yourself. You don't deceive me,' Diana said coolly.

Paul laughed without humour. 'Ah, as they say, mothers are people with x-ray eyes. They are the first ones to find out what you don't want anyone to know.'

Although many children complied with parental demands, her only child didn't often do so graciously. Diana wondered if all the years Paul had seemed like he was following her wishes instead of rebelling, he was hanging onto the resentment that had turned him into the person he was today. Paul hated living in Africa and marrying Mollie had been one of his achievements in showing that he didn't care much for Africa and the family business. It was like the concepts of every game. You had the chances to win or lose, what wasn't only certain were the odds.

Dr Domboka begged Ruvimbo to soften up and accept what had happened. He convinced her to meet Tendai's fiancé. The dinner was prepared by an anxious Mrs Domboka who knew that her niece was a good person, but when it came to being expressive on personal views, Ruvimbo wasn't one who held back what she thought.

Ruvimbo chose to arrive when she was sure that everyone else was at Uncle Francis's house. She met Kudakwashe for the first time and was touched. He was an entertaining young man who had an enchanting smile. He wasn't shy and his self-confidence was appealing to Ruvimbo. The big sister had to admit grudgingly that Tendai had made a good choice.

'Tell me something, *Amaiguru* – how do you live with yourself?'

'Excuse me?' Ruvimbo said, confused.

Kuda laughed. 'You are the one behind the idea of a modern day sovereign woman. The women in my home village are constantly holding the men there responsible for massive gender inequality.'

Ruvimbo smiled. 'The world is changing, *Babamunini*. What used to be no longer is anymore.'

'But our culture is still the same,' Tendai said. 'I hoped some of it would change.'

'Some of it, like what?' Mrs Domboka asked.

'Things like *kuperekwa* and stuff.'

Mrs Domboka understood instantly and laughed. 'You aren't going to get out of that one, *muzukuru*. You better prepare for it because *vekuGuruve ndivo vanonzi vanhu vakudhara chaivo*.'

'Pardon me, Aunt, but we are ordinary people who follow cultural rules no matter how much soap you give us to wash our black skin white.'

Everyone laughed merrily. 'You too, Ruvimbo, you'll be in line hand in hand with your sister when the time comes,' Mrs Domboka added.

'That will be the highlight of my life,' Dr Domboka said. 'CEO of WT accompanying her young sister to the rural of all rural areas to serve old *madharas* bathing water from the river.'

More laughter filled the house. Ruvimbo was suddenly aware of how serious this was. She was going to do something she had never done or seen before. Her deceased sister or cousins had never been married and that traditional part of her culture had somehow skipped her. She was so used to town life now that the countryside would be foreign to her. There was no escaping this responsibility for she was the only sister. Tendai had made two records in their Domboka generation. She had become the first to obtain a doctorate as a woman and the first to get married. Ruvimbo was happy for her sister and vowed to help her in any way she could to live her dreams.

That night, she left for her home and slept soundly. She woke up at midnight feeling hot. Memories of the day started to playback in her mind. A wave of sudden sadness spread through her as she thought of her own life. *Was she happy?* No she wasn't. For someone who had almost everything money could buy, she felt bad for what she didn't have. Normally, she would have been married by now with one or two children. Instead, she was alone and had a vendetta to conclude.

Paul found his new mistress desirable every time they got together. The odd thing about it though was that Ruvimbo always found an excuse not to sleep with him anymore. An affair that lacked any sexual intercourse much to his frustration. He tried to be patient with her and socialized with her to buy off time. He however discovered less than what he would have wanted to know about Ruvimbo.

With time, Paul learned that Ruvimbo never talked about her parents or past. When he had asked, she had simply told him that they had died. He hadn't asked her anything about her unknown family again. After all, he wasn't planning on marrying her, was he?

'When that nice black girl finds out about what you really are, son, you'll regret it,' Diana advised him. 'I wouldn't get too close with her if I were you.'

'Why do you care, mother? You hate all of them,' Paul replied

'That woman has been the engine and brains to the success of WT. She is black, yes, I admit, but I don't have to like her to respect her.'

Paul grinned. 'Well, that is a first. Cancer has really done something to your heartless persona.'

'Ruvimbo is a good person, you never will be. She wasn't born for your soiled soul, Paul – leave her alone,' Diana's voice was annoyingly even.

'You lived your own life, made your own mistakes and paid for them fully,' Paul said. 'Let me live mine.'

'You made your bed and you'll have to lie in it,' Diana said and left him.

Time passed and Paul avoided his mother as long as he could. It was now in December and the environment was all about Christmas. Heaven's Ministry held many charity events based on fundraising money for the needy and old. WT backed out at the last moment and Paul was much seethed. Diana knew what this act would do to the Ministry and Paul knew that his mother was going down with a fight.

'I don't believe you did this!' Paul screamed at her. She was sitting in the sun, enjoying the fresh air with a glass of cool lemonade by her side. 'Even you can't sink so low. This is charity works, damnit!'

Diana was unmoved. 'Who cares, it's not my race, not my problem. It is your church, isn't it?'

'You are so evil, you don't deserve to live!'

'If I'm supposed to die because I am evil, then what can we say about you, Paul?' Diana replied smoothly. 'After all that you have done, do you truly deserve to live?'

Paul snorted and walked away. His mother knew *something*. The problem was actually guessing what she knew for she hadn't told him yet, if ever. He played it safe by not confronting Diana than was necessary.

If Diana suddenly told Ruvimbo whatever she knew, Paul knew that he would miss all that pleasure. His past was a chain of unforgivable sins, sins he couldn't erase.

Chapter 7

Kudakwashe Chuma came from a well up family. His father was a Minister in the government. The mother was a senior nurse and he was the last-born child in a family of four children.

The Chumas supported Kudakwashe's marriage to Tendai. They even supported his notion for an early wedding date, which was ultimately set to be on the 23rd of December, if the other traditional rituals were to be fulfilled by then.

Mrs Domboka accompanied her urban-bred nieces to the rural areas of Guruve where Tendai was going to be officially accepted into the Chumas' family. Kudakwashe used his father's SUV to transport them there and they arrived at five in the evening.

'Is this far enough?' he asked the more experienced woman of the lot.

Mrs Domboka assessed the area and nodded. 'I think so, we need to suck your people as much money as possible,' she said climbing out of the front of the car.

Ruvimbo and Tendai, who were sitting in the back, laughed nervously. The three women were all wearing long African cloths called *mazambia* together with small colourful cloths covering their hair. Kudakwashe left them at the edge of the village and went to inform his relatives that *varoora* had arrived.

'This is going to be something really,' Ruvimbo said, estimating the distance they were going to crawl until they reached the final destination.

They were going to be involved in a Shona ritual called *kuperekwa kwemuroora.* This ritual was composed of an act where the bride to be and her sisters were welcomed into the groom's family. It was a very interesting ritual for, at first the *muroora* and her escorts were to be covered from head to toe with a huge cloth so that nobody could see them. Mrs Domboka was to act as the guide and director of the ladies' movements. The bride and sister were to crawl or move only if the groom's family gave them money for each movement, in other terms, some sort of payment.

'I'm very nervous,' Tendai shook from under the cloth.

'Save it for later!' Ruvimbo whispered back.

They could barely see anything from under the cloth, but they could hear the crowd approaching. From the noise they made, the Chumas were indeed a noisy few.

The ritual began by the Chumas greeting the *varoora* with song and dance. The Domboka sisters trembled under the cloth not knowing how to react. They waited for the pre-given signals from their aunt. Ten minutes passed and the two thought for a second that Mrs Domboka had fled the scene. The first signal came two minutes later. They crawled on the long cloth Mrs Domboka had rolled on the hard surface for two meters before the stop signal was given.

Ruvimbo felt her knees hot. She had never crawled on a surface of any nature for God knew how long. She was a businessperson not a general worker. What had seemed easy was turning to be a feat of strength.

More cheers came from the crowd. Some of them were in no mood to hang around all evening so they tried to mock the unseen *varoora* in an attempt to intimidate them so they could move.

'Okay, we don't have any more money,' one shouted.

'Let's leave them alone, the hyenas will get them soon if they don't move. It's just about that time they start patrolling. Let's go!' Another female added.

'Hyenas?' Tendai panicked.

The two under the veil heard the crowd leave like a sound of an ocean wave. Silenced followed.

'What's going on out there, Aunt?' Ruvimbo whispered, anxious to the bone.

'They have gone – all of them,' Mrs Domboka responded in an unbelievably calm voice.

'What?' Tendai said, almost taking the veil off. Her mind was set on hyenas.

'They just left us out here?' Ruvimbo was awed.

'Calm down, relax. These people are very clever,' Mrs Domboka chuckled richly. 'They know who you are and will try to use that to their advantage. It's the first time I've seen this – psychological tactics and they surely planned for it.'

'Psychological tactics?' Tendai asked.

'They will come back, don't worry,' Mrs Domboka reassured them.

'What about the hyenas?'

'I can't believe someone as smart as you could fall for that,' the experienced woman replied. 'They took a gamble with the wrong person here.'

'What do you mean?' Ruvimbo closed her eyes to accustom them to the dark interior.

'They wanted to scare us so that when they return they will easily persuade us to move no matter how much they throw at us. I'm going to make them pay big time for this.'

'How much have you got now?' Ruvimbo was curious.

'Three hundred dollars,' Mrs Domboka said proudly. It was a lot of money to get from only a few meters of movement. No wonder the Chumas had tried to unnerve them. 'And here they come.'

The Chumas returned an animated lot. Some of them must have gulped down some traditional beer to psyche themselves up because they were louder than ever. They however realized that they had provoked the wrong birds for Mrs Domboka didn't budge until they had sourced out another three hundred dollars.

Ruvimbo and Tendai crawled for another few meters, shorter than the first movements. The Chumas cried foul, but as silent as she was, Mrs Domboka stood her ground.

When the Chumas realized that they weren't going to get it any easier, they generously emptied their pockets and after five hundred good dollars, bruised shins and knees for the *varoora* and their aunt, they finally ended up in the main house which was diversified from the many huts that occupied the area.

'If we paid that much to get them in here, what will we pay them to make them unveil?' one of Kuda's uncles asked the others, away from the *varoora's* hearing.

'I do hope we hadn't tried that trick,' a lady said to the gathering as they planned on how to progress.

'It worked on you, didn't it?' Kudakwashe's mother teased.

The group dispersed after a while, anticipating the worst. Many were going to come out very broke from the ritual.

Kudakwashe's mother went to look for his father and found her husband enjoying himself with his brothers around a fire drinking the beer he had bought from the city.

'*BaKuda*, we need some more money *tifugure muroora*,' she said kneeling.

BaKuda laughed as if it was a joke. 'What for? Those Dombokas don't need money. They have a lot of it.'

'It's not about them having money. I think you know what I mean,' Mrs Chuma said.

After a couple of minutes, she came out with the money she wanted from all of them. She left them to drink their beer peacefully as they discussed politics.

Four hundred dollars is what it took to unveil the two sisters simultaneously. The house being adequately equipped with electricity, as it belonged to a high ranked government official, was well lit – inside and out. Many thought it was the light playing tricks with hem.

'Are they coloureds?' some whispered in the crowd.

The beauty of the Domboka sisters, especially Ruvimbo who they confused to be the bride, tuned the Chumas into a few minutes of whispers and frequent silence. The money they had all contributed, as expensive as it was, was all forgotten for the moment it had all been meant for overrode its value.

Ruvimbo stared down nervously as she felt their eyes on them.

It was a very uncomfortable moment and she wished she were anywhere else, but there. She had been a lawyer, was now a CEO who dealt with crowds of people almost on a weekly basis, but this was different. Tendai was beyond nervousness. The only person who looked calm and composed was their aunt. *Why couldn't she?* She had just made a personal record – and who knew where else – by milking a family about one thousand six hundred dollars for *kuperekwa kwemuroora*.

Fifty dollars was paid for them to open their mouths and Ruvimbo and Tendai acted their part by greeting the Chumas as they had been endlessly taught and rehearsed by their aunt the previous days. Mrs Domboka first started by introducing herself then her nieces. She distinguished the bride for them and, although Tendai didn't look as perfect as Ruvimbo, they were overjoyed. When they introduced themselves, the sisters brought more whispers.

Ruvimbo's accent caught their full awareness. Having a British accent and using her mother's language at the same time was the highlight of the introductions. Most who knew who she was for real weren't that much surprised, but were awed to see her in person. They knew that it was entirely her choice to participate when she could have done something else with her time. The women who knew what she stood for had nothing, but royal respect for her.

The day was a Friday that ended well and the exhausted sisters slept without dreaming that night. When Saturday came, the sisters were thankful for their aunt's foresight. She hadn't made the Chumas pay all that cash for nothing. As the new *varoora*, they were scheduled to sweep the Chumas' village yard and provide the whole family with the ritual bathing water.

'This is torture,' Ruvimbo complained as they swept the yards that had a lot of leaves.

'I think these leaves were purposefully left to accumulate for us to sweep,' Tendai noted.

As they did their chores, Kudakwashe and his brother fetched water for them from a nearby borehole. It was a lucky thing they did so because the women were expected to do these tasks on their own.

Eyes were hot on them, especially the beautiful sister. Her skin was so smooth and spotless many thought she was going to be torn apart like a piece of paper.

'*Muzukuru*, if you could just ask those boys to collect wood for us to make fire later for boiling the water,' Mrs Domboka said, smiling at Ruvimbo.

Ruvimbo looked at the boys in question and saw them staring. They were absolutely enchanted by her appearance. 'We are allowed to do that?' she asked.

'There are no rules that say we can't.'

'Wouldn't they oblige if the ask came from someone like you?' Ruvimbo wasn't keen to the idea. 'I mean someone older and respectable.'

Mrs Domboka laughed. 'Word around everyone here has it that I'm the hardheaded aunt who isn't somebody one can talk to without expecting me to be stern. You – on the other hand, believe me, they wouldn't refuse.'

'Why?' Tendai didn't understand.

'Because your sister looks like an Angel cut from a fairy-tale book,' Mrs Domboka said, snatching the *mutsvairo* from her niece. She pushed Ruvimbo towards the boys.

Ruvimbo had no choice, but to do as asked. Her anxiety increased with every step she took. *Now I am scared of teenage boys*, she thought annoyed of herself for being weak. The boys didn't move as they watched her walk towards them as if they were a deer in front of a car's headlight.

'That wasn't too hard, was it?' Mrs Domboka said later, watching the boys fight over carrying the perfect firewood for the fire.

Ruvimbo's stomach churned and she felt clammy for a while. 'I feel sick,' she complained her hand on her belly.

'It's just the environment, a big change from Harare,' Mrs Domboka said confidently.

The day seemed to be the longest day of the Domboka sisters. Their aunt, who made sure that they appeared extremely tired in order to satisfy the Chumas, worked them hard. The Chumas were indeed a lovely family. They were like every other family, meaning they all had problems of their own, but they were united that day. They wanted their new daughter-in-law to feel special and welcomed into their family. Even those who had grievances against each other held hands in cheering.

Ruvimbo's stomach made a nuisance of itself that night and the following day. She threw up a lot and she assumed that it was either the food they ate or the country's air. It was embarrassing to be found ill at such a moment, so she masked on a brave face.

Back home – that Sunday's evening – she went straight to bed after finding some small letters Paul had left her that weekend. He wanted to see her as soon as possible and Ruvimbo could only guess correctly why. Their affair, be it for attraction, lust or love was floating to great heights. Ruvimbo knew that she couldn't carry on the relationship because she was afraid she would slip one day and sleep with Paul. Paul already had *Istreblyat'* now, although it hadn't started attacking him, and she had to be careful not to catch it from him. This was the first time she was dealing with a situation where she was seeing the person she had injected with the virus, after she had done it. All her other victims had been one-offs to worry about contracting the virus from them in whatever way the virus spread. One thing she was confident though by now was that the virus was transmitted almost the same way AIDS did – through blood.

She was sure that the job was done and that she needed to worry about Paul's children next. The sons were Westwoods and that meant they had to suffer the fate of their name.

Ruvimbo wondered if her weekend's sickness was more than just a small reaction to change in scenery or food. She visited her private doctor the next day and waited for the results.

'I'm sorry, Ms Domboka, but did you know that you are HIV positive?' the doctor said with a sad face. *How could such an attractive successful nice lady have the deadly virus?* He had rechecked the results hoping for a false positive and had come out with the same results.

Ruvimbo's expression didn't change. She had slept with many white men before she had injected them with *Istreblyat'*. It was no surprise she had a sexually transmitted virus.

'I do know, doctor.'

The doctor was a bit socked. He often hated telling people that they had HIV, but this was unexpected. The young lady wasn't reacting as he had expected she would.

'Did you also know that you are pregnant?'

'What?' Ruvimbo cried.

This was the reaction the doctor had expected from the start. He finally had it.

Part Two

Paul

April 2002 – Gweru, Harare

Chapter 8

The Westwood family was amongst the first settlers to colonize Rhodesia and had survived the first Chimurenga. They had settled near Gwelo for a long time before moving up north to what was now Kadoma. The family tree bloomed well and the generations had developed remarkably. The first war however disintegrated that structure and left less than five original Westwood sons.

One son left the country towards Boers' land when the gold and diamond rush begun. The remaining three had increased their share of space by invading more land. Frequent uprisings killed one of the Rhodesian Westwoods and the surviving two had taken over his land. One was the Westwood who had occupied the land that was adjacent to the Dombokas' village. His name was called Jorum Westwood.

Jorum had loathed the natives, but not as much as he had loathed his brother who had died in the war. The brother had been the eldest and a controlling maniac. His death was a blessing in disguise for Jorum instantaneously salvaged the immaculate lands he had left behind.

Much to his dismay, Jorum's first child had been a girl. He desired as many heirs as possible and the arrival of another daughter had only made him more aggressive. His wish was granted on the third try, but that also came with a price. The last birth was so complex for his wife that she was unable to conceive again.

The first few years of Jorum's venture as a farmer paid off mainly because of the free labour he received from the natives.

Nevertheless, the British and Russian missionaries that had settled haphazardly close to the land he had inherited gave him a lot of emotional trouble when it came to how he was supposed to treat the natives. Despite all this tension, he had managed to carry out his services without any physical confrontation from either party.

When Jorum's other brother, Timothy, had a son called Paul in 1963, Jorum was on the brink of production success. His native neighbours were helpful in the stressful agricultural seasons and he had pulled through by imitating their methods.

The seventies began and ended badly for Jorum. He was involved with the deaths of almost the entire Dombokas' family. He too lost his whole family except his only son, Frank. Unable to live with his grief, Jorum had succumbed to heavy drinking and suffocated to death one afternoon.

Paul Westwood's father died in 1995 and left him the house in Harare. Paul had let his mother be the caretaker of the house for the first few months until he officially became the owner and President of the family's company after his father.

Paul had lived a pretty complex life from the age of twenty-five. He had left the country when he had turned eighteen to pursue his higher education in England. Three years and a half had been like a fairy-tale. His childhood in Rhodesia had been dramatic. He was the only child and the dream of being the only was vaporized when his parents had expected nothing, but a perfect boy.

Paul didn't care much about his family's history. What intrigued him though was how his favourite uncle had returned from Southern Rhodesia with a fortune to form a very lucrative huge company called Westwood Company. He barely heard of his other uncles' scandals and failures. His father had made sure of it. Their first house had been in Kwekwe near Kadoma. Later they moved to Gwelo, which to date was now Gweru, where they settled for more than fifteen years.

Paul's childhood was affected when his mother left for England when he was nine years old. When she returned three years later, Paul had lost that special connection with his mother to care much about her. Diana always complained that her son never listened to her. She was twenty-eight years old when she had had Paul. Her pregnancy had been very difficult and she was ill most of the time. Paul's father, at the time, had resented her pregnancy. He personally thought having a child that early in life was going to hinder his progress as an employee at the Westwood Company.

From Paul's birth, Diana and her husband couldn't do any of the things they used to do together. Timothy stayed away more and more from Gwelo and buried himself in the family business. He became remote and growing up, Paul became very sensitive.

Paul despised the lack of positive strokes from his parents as he grew older. He was reared in a fourteen-roomed house on a two-acre plot of ground very isolated from the few white neighbours they had. He saw his parents as cool and aloof. They never displayed spontaneous bursts of affection and, since he grew up seeing his mother more, he saw his father as a stranger.

'Public display of emotions is in poor state, son,' his father would say. 'Don't hug me every time I come back from Salisbury.'

Diana fooled herself thinking that her child liked to be teased. The few years she had lost in England made her misinterpret Paul's aloofness for being a self-sufficient boy who had made it for three years without mummy. Paul put up with it, accommodating his parents' need for a hostility release. His hunger for parental attention waned off when he became a teenager. Most of his time was spent with his private tutor who was secretly more imbued to religious ethics than he let Paul's parents see. Paul found peace by reading and criticizing the Bible and the human race. He physically and psychological withdrew himself from his parents and threw himself into fantasies.

Timothy bought a mine in Shamva when he became the President of Westwood Company after his famous brother and founder of the company was attacked and killed during the Second Chimurenga. Unfortunately, the brother had been travelling with his family that day and the reigns to the Westwood Company were automatically thrust into Timothy's hands. It was an uncontested pass over for the other closely related Westwoods spread throughout the country were less keen to compete for the position knowing that the owner and family were killed for no other reason, but their connection to the company. Westwood Company was accused of aiding the British soldiers, in that case the Rhodesian Army, in fighting the Resistance of the guerrilla fighters.

The first thing Timothy did when he became the President of the company was to disassociate it from politics. The Rhodesian Army wasn't too happy about this, but they had the Resistance to worry about more than the defection of a business that was developed from their corruption.

When the Westwoods saw that their son was very intelligent, they sent him to England for university. Reluctant to leave newly independent Zimbabwe, at first afraid of the change that was going to come with it, Paul had found himself not wanting to return.

The life Paul Westwood lived in England transformed him from being withdrawn from social interactions to a cunning adult. He was accepted socially and respected by his peers because of his family's achievements down South. He adapted to the family's script, which was perpetuated by the *"We Westwoods have always been cut above others"* phrase.

Three years and so passed and Timothy summoned his son back home to work for the family business. Paul brought back home a present.

'I'm not really surprised. It was inevitable,' his mother had said. 'We send you for education and you bring us back a baron's daughter.'

It wasn't what she said that angered Paul, it was the way Diana had said it. What he didn't know was that Diana had been personally violated because her only child had married someone and she hadn't known or been present at the ceremony.

The Westwoods' surname reflected the family's heritage and gave some unpleasant cultural scripting to everyone who was involved. Paul was so closely identified with his family's name that he had learned to use it almost exclusively.

From the word go, Diana and Molline Grant didn't like each other. Diana was more annoyed because the girl had grown in a wealthy and influential family to succumb to her control. Mollie was stubborn and didn't give her mother-in-law the respect Diana thought she deserved.

Timothy sold the mine and used some of the money to build a mansion in Harare. A year later, he moved to Harare leaving his Gweru house to his son. Mollie was happy to see her mother-in-law leave, but was stunned when her husband formed a church couple of years later finally living one of his childhood fantasies.

Heaven's Ministry was born for a particular reason and that was to convert the local blacks from their traditional flawed misguided ways to a clean life. Paul saw himself as a prophet whose purpose in life was to change the lives of the race he called "the darkened race". In life, sacrifices had to be made to achieve certain goals.

Paul loved to read the scriptures of Leviticus that focused on guilt offering.

> *If a person sins and is unfaithful to the Lord by deceiving his neighbours about something entrusted to him or left in his care or stolen, or if he cheats him, or if he finds lost property and lies about it, or if he swears falsely, or if he commits any such sin that people may do - he must make restitution in full.*

Paul felt like he needed to atone for the atrocities the Westwood generations had committed. The loveless lives his ancestors had lived had to be *cleansed.*

The moment he formed Heaven's Ministry, he had begun his quest of making guilt sacrifices. He saw himself as Abraham – and was glorified by his actions. The sacrifices started two years after the church was formed and it was fully functional. What triggered the reaction was the conversation he had had with his father, then mother, when he had visited them at their Harare home.

'A church, son?' Timothy said looking pale. Age had caught up with him. 'You are full of surprises.'

Paul didn't take much notice of his father's sarcasm. 'Yes, father, I started a church to make this country a better place to live,' he said.

'You are heir of Westwood Company and what do you do with your money and spare time? You start a bloody church, how wise.'

Paul frowned displeased. 'At least if I'm to ever have children one day, they won't grow up to be immoral twats.'

'And what's that supposed to mean?' Timothy said.

'You don't fool me, father, you have been having affair after affair. People see things and talk.'

'Gossip isn't for men, son, it makes them weak,' Timothy said coldly.

The following evening, Paul came across his mother sitting on the garden's table staring absently at the pond. 'Are you okay, mother?' he asked.

'Just thinking, dear,' Diana said.

Paul was surprised to see her actually thinking and not eating. His mother had learned to take her mind off problems by stuffing her stomach with food. She had grown huge over the years, which showed that her worries never seemed to end.

'Are you worried about father?' he asked.

'Your father cheats on me every day, why should I worry about him?' Diana mumbled.

'You know about his insecurities?' Paul was stunned. 'Well – I…' he couldn't finish.

'Don't be sorry for me, Paul,' Diana said. 'I was foolish enough to get involved with this family. The Westwoods are genetically cruel and evil.'

Paul returned to Gweru disturbed in every manner. He read the Bible and came across the scriptures of Abraham and his son Isaac. He found a youthful black boy and, in the middle of the night, *sacrificed* him to the Lord. That was only the start. Whenever he felt like he had to cleanse the family's guilt from his soul, he searched for, found a young boy, and gave him to the Lord.

Chapter 9

It was on the 3rd of March 2002, fourteen and so years since Heaven's Ministry was created, when Paul commemorated its birth by holding a big function at his Gweru's house. Many guests appeared and he let his Mollie worry about the hospitality whilst he searched for a new *sacrifice*.

As he looked around, he spotted the ideal candidate. He went over and introduced himself. Mollie watched from afar and frowned.

'How long have you been a member of the church, Saint?' Paul asked, putting his charm.

The young man was awed at being approached by the owner of the church. 'Two years since I finished school and heard the Lord calling me.'

Paul smiled disarmingly and started to talk about Gospels. The young man listened surprised at the knowledge Paul Westwood possessed.

'Are you from around Gweru?'

'No, sir,' the young man relied. 'I am from Mbare – Harare.'

'Do you work?'

'Yes, sir, I work at a retail outlet.'

Paul noticed the fresh look in the boy's eyes and estimated that he was older than he looked. 'Would you like to work for the Church of God?'

'I'd be honoured, sir,' the boy couldn't hide his excitement.

'Come and see me two days from now and I'll see if we can get you a higher paying and purposeful position, Saint.'

Paul delayed his return to Harare by three days so he could help this young man. A day later, he met the young man, he returned to Harare satisfied.

Mr Grant of *Grant and Associates* had lunch with one of his employees that month and came out with an idea. He met with his cousin Mollie who was married to the President of Westwood Company. Mollie was ecstatic about the idea and she presented the idea to her husband. The name of the project was to be called *Women of Tomorrow*.

At the time facing charges for bribing shareholders of a few local companies in an attempt to acquire their businesses, most of them being women, Paul readily gave in to the idea. Mr Grant offered his talented young female associate to Paul, advising him that she was the perfect person to lead the project. Paul read Ruvimbo Domboka's profile and came out satisfied.

Days later, he met Ruvimbo in person.

'Did you see her?' Mollie asked the night Ruvimbo had paid Paul a visit.

'Yes, she is the right person for the job,' Paul replied, getting ready to leave for an evening party one of his company's executives was holding.

'What do you mean the right person?'

'She is black, young, intelligent and confident.'

Mollie pinned her earing the wrong way and took it off frustrated. 'And beautiful as well?' she said.

'I wouldn't know.'

'You are really like your father, Paul,' Mollie said angrily. 'Your mother warned me about your kind.'

'My mother is a selfish hypocrite, since when did you start listening to her silly ideologies?' Paul asked.

'Since I started opening my eyes and saw that she was correct,' Mollie heated up. 'Do you deny having an affair with your accountant's wife and his sister at the same time?'

Paul didn't answer. He felt like giving another sacrifice and that meant returning to Gweru. He fought his desires, knowing that if he lost control of the situation, the authorities were going to find out about his sacrifices.

'What's the matter?'

'It's nothing,' Paul muttered. 'Forget it.'

'Good Lord!' Mollie exclaimed, rising off her dressing table.

'I'll meet you downstairs – if you ever finish getting yourself ready,' Paul replied leaving the bedroom feeling defensive.

They left the kids with their grandmother and Mollie felt uncomfortable that evening knowing that her husband was truly having multi-affairs like her mother-in-law had taunted her.

Mollie had fallen in love with Paul because he had been a very charming young man when they had met at Portsmouth University. The daughter of an industrialist, she had demanded and got the best things in life. Having it all, the beauty and the money wasn't enough for her. She was born an adventurer who liked to explore life and its meaning. Most of all, she loved nature. Snowy days in England had made her full of bliss. The sunny days, as few as they were, had filled her with warmth.

Mollie had studied History and Arts at Portsmouth University and had coincidentally bumped into Paul who was majoring in Economics. Instantly consumed by the handsome Westwood and his well up social identity at the campus, she had readily accepted his proposal for marriage after they had graduated. The Baron had approved the marriage despite the absence of Paul's parents who were said to be bravely fighting post-war oppressions back home.

Expecting their son-in-law to stay in England till the trouble home was over, the Baron gave Paul a piece of their own land and a house. Knowing very well that he was expected back home as soon as possible, Paul coerced Mollie to elope with him without her parents' knowledge. The adventure, thrill-loving Mollie had agreed and not a minute passed did she not regret her mistake as they drove to the party.

Mollie wanted to leave Paul to return to England, but the two children she had suddenly had over the past few years bound her against leaving. She tolerated her husband for the sake of her young children. The adventure she had anticipated she would live had only been there when she had arrived in Zimbabwe in the eighties. It hadn't lasted long.

When Mr Grant had approached her with the idea of forming Women of Tomorrow using the Westwoods' name and influence, Mollie saw her escape towards being an independent woman.

During that week, Paul gave her the Women of Tomorrow legal papers to sign. Mollie was appalled because she was the last person to sign them, not to mention that Paul didn't take the innovation seriously.

'What has Heaven's Ministry got to do with WT?' she asked when she finished reading the contract.

'It's a lure to WT, it will act as a conduit,' Paul explained. 'Please – don't worry, dear. Nothing out of the ordinary will happen.'

'I hope so, Paul,' Mollie said and signed the papers. She was yet to meet the chosen CEO. 'When will I meet this Ms Domboka?'

Paul shrugged. 'As soon as you want, Mollie.'

'Mum is calling her a black-British – what's that supposed to mean?'

Paul laughed. His mother had a way with words. 'Ms Domboka possesses a British accent and the hair of an African American,' he explained.

'I can't wait to meet her now,' Mollie smiled back.

Mollie finally met Ruvimbo during the pre-opening ceremony of WT. Ruvimbo's appearance made her envy her. She was African, but looked African American. Mollie didn't have anything against the African race, so she started by being amiable and sociable towards her CEO.

'You were once a lawyer, Ms Domboka?' Mollie checked.

Ruvimbo smiled at her. She liked the way this Mrs Westwood went about herself.

'I was and I think this job is going to be very challenging than my prior occupation,' she said.

'I hope not, we need you.'

'WT was your idea, I heard,' Ruvimbo said. 'A very smart one if I must say, Mrs Westwood.'

'Oh, thank you,' Mollie beamed proudly. 'Oh, no, here comes Diana.'

The two women watched uneasily as Diana walked to them carrying a nearly empty wine glass.

'So you two have met. My ambitious daughter, what do you think of our new African friend?'

Ruvimbo inwardly admired Diana for her nerve. She looked sober and alert for someone who had consumed more than five glasses of wine that evening.

'Her name is Ms Domboka, Mum, for Christ's sake behave,' Mollie snapped at her.

'I'll leave you two to it then,' Diana said and left the two women watching her go.

'Forgive her. She has a very bad attitude plus a daring mouth,' Mollie apologized. She giggled as she watched one of their guests flee from Diana.

'She speaks her mind,' Ruvimbo said. Diana must have heard these words for she stared back at them and raised a new glass of white wine to them.

Mollie scanned Ruvimbo's fingers and was curious enough to ask. 'Are you married?'

'No,' Ruvimbo replied simply. 'My work hasn't given me much room to occupy a relationship, a serious one I mean.'

'Lucky you,' Mollie said.

The two women instantly became odd friends. They spent the following days strategizing about WT and its motives. Ruvimbo let Mollie detect the flaws that were going to arise if WT was to be hugely connected with Heaven's Ministry. It was better for Mollie to do it herself so that she would approach her husband unbiased from external views. Mollie dictated the flow of WT's progress to the day it started to become famous.

The first argument appeared when one of WT's executive members corrupted the whole recruitment system. The organization had been created to accommodate only female members and potential members had to come from all backgrounds. The selection was however subjective because the top management chose members according to race and if you weren't part of Heaven's Ministry, your chances of becoming a WT member were very slim. Discovering this made Ruvimbo aware of how powerless her presumed elite position was.

Mollie knew that the CEO was right, but she didn't want to seem weak to those members who supported her. These members were high up there in the corruption zone. She planned to warn them to play it low because she knew that Ruvimbo wasn't going to back down. Mollie had studied her CEO meticulously and she knew that crossing her would be a big mistake.

Chapter 10

Ruvimbo presented her issue once again when the situation worsened. African ladies were paying her numerous visits, complaining about the unfair selection of WT members. This time she did it systematically. She got her co-bosses together in the same room and was open to them about how she felt about the current problems.

'She has a point, you know,' Paul said when they were alone at home.

'Don't you think I know that, Paul?' Mollie cried. 'The problem is your church people.'

'My church people?'

'Yes, Paul, yesterday you returned from Gweru suggesting that WT be more connected to the church,' Mollie said. 'What was that all about?'

Paul ignored his wife. He had just made another sacrifice the day before the prior one. It was a fourteen-year-old homeless boy this time. Counting them, they were now more than ten sacrifices since the formation of the church.

So far, he had operated unnoticed, but at the moment he was curious about his mother. She had a cunning way of wanting to know things whenever she became suspicious.

The argument between his wife and Ruvimbo had caused a headache and listening to his wife bickering didn't do any good.

'Okay, deal with it however you want,' he said and gulped a glass full of water after taking some aspirin.

He wished he had sacrificed his quarrelsome wife instead to save himself from the misery. *Better to live on a corner of the roof than share a house with a quarrelsome wife*, he re-quote Proverbs in his head.

To regain her CEO's trust, Mollie fired a few of the corrupt executive members of WT. Ruvimbo appreciated the gesture by accepting Mollies frequent dinner visits. Ruvimbo found out why it was so easy for Mollie to fire the culprits. Paul had left for South Africa on business. They had no idea when he was going to return and Mollie didn't care. The two of them had automatically withdrawn from themselves into open relationships. Mollie no longer slept in the same bed with her husband. She was aware of the sexually transmitted diseases that were currently a nuisance and she played it safe.

Paul returned home after three weeks. He was exhausted from travelling. He had been in South Africa, Mozambique and Zambia where he had been required to see how the other Westwood Company branches sited there were coping. Mollie barely took notice of him. She was always drowned in paperwork for WT and was very angered when disturbed. Paul had satisfied his sexual desires elsewhere.

On the other hand, Mollie wanted to show Paul that she was just as smart and capable as he was at running a business. Paul's sudden loss of interest in WT pleased her a little. She was doing it all on her own. That meant she was succeeding.

Paul accompanied his mother to Kwekwe to see his cousin brother who was dangerously ill. Cousin Frank Westwood was in his early forties and well known for his insatiable appetite for women. Paul liked Frank because he was one of the few Westwood sons who hadn't fallen into the trap of the family business. Frank was a free agent who had made his own money and exceled in life without the help of the family name. Frank was one of the small number of Westwood boys Diana adored and when the news that he was seriously out of health reached Harare, Diana had chosen the day her daughter-in-law was opening a WT branch in Karoi as the appropriate day to visit Frank.

'You did this on purpose, mother,' Paul said as he drove to Frank's house.

'Of course, I chose Mollie's great day to be absent,' Diana said lazing in the back seat. 'You know me well, son.'

'What an honest answer.'

'An honest answer is like a kiss on the lips,' Diana said. 'Even the Bible said it.'

Paul was amused that such a contemptuous woman could even have time to read a sentence or phrase in the Bible 'You have to let go of some things, mother,' he said firmly.

'Like you do? Why do you keep returning to that old house in Gweru? Are you letting go of your first home?'

Paul grunted. If his mother knew why he made trips to and from Gweru, he was confident that she would die sooner of a heart attack no matter how strong-willed she was.

'I've businesses in Gweru. Heaven's Ministry's Headquarters is there,' he said defending himself.

The two Westwoods didn't speak to each other for the rest of the journey. Diana's mind was busy dreaming of all the nice food she had packed for her favourite nephew whilst Paul thought of how angry Mollie was because he wasn't at WT Karoi's opening.

Cousin Frank looked like a skeleton. His young wife of two years of marriage looked happy to see them arrive, but deep down she was destroyed. The disease was eating Frank alive and she was very afraid that she too was going to be affected by it soon.

Paul looked sadly at Frank who was covered in blankets in an attempt to keep him warm on a sunny day. What didn't change on his cousin was his forever-smiling face. Paul stayed by his bedside as the ladies comforted each other in the kitchen where they prepared food in efforts to keep their minds off Frank's condition.

'You don't look so good, man,' Paul said.

'I don't think I've much time left, Paul – my days are numbered,' Frank's voice sounded like a rasped whisper.

'Hang in there, brother.'

'I wish I could, but this AIDS thing is no joke,' Frank said. 'This is the punishment for all those men who go around and can't keep their instruments in their pants.'

'Didn't you always say *rubber* was the getaway? What happened, Frank?' Paul wanted to know.

Frank coughed and it took him a minute to recover and get his breath back. 'I met someone who looked beyond anything I had ever seen. She was the best at everything. I think if I didn't give her the disease, she must have been the one who gave it to me. That was one of the few times I didn't use rubbers and those were the worst and last mistakes of my life.'

Paul drove his mother back home the following day planning to go back to Gweru to make another sacrifice as soon as possible. What he had seen had scared the wits out of him. He couldn't shake off the tremors he was experiencing. Even his hard-core mother didn't look so composed.

'It won't be long till you become the last Westwood of your generation, Paul.' Diana said.

Many Westwoods had died over the past few years and – one way or the other – she knew it wasn't a coincidence that they had died in almost similar fashions. Paul said nothing for the whole journey back to Harare.

The month of July was spent on sleepless nights for Mollie. She was left with Diana at the house as Paul was out of the country, again. Mollie focused all her attention on WT's new branch, which was being set up in Victoria Falls. As a major tourist destination, Mollie and Ruvimbo planned it to be bigger and stylish.

For the project to prosper, the ladies had to acquire the help of Heaven's Ministry. The church was very influential in that region and for WT to come out best, the intervention of the church was inevitable. With Paul out of the country, Mollie took that advantage and lured the church members of Vic Falls into quickly facilitating her plans. The members obliged without any queries. The wife of their leader was just as good as the leader himself.

Diana turned to her grandchildren for comfort. The house was a bore, it lacked activity and she didn't find herself useful. Her grandsons spent most of their time with her for their mother was a very busy woman. Diana finally recognized the traits, the love the children desired and lacked from their parents. She saw her mistakes with Paul and regretted having made his son become what he was today. She took the boys to Gweru to relive her memories and show them where their father had once lived. Her stay was cut short when she discovered things that nearly made her heart stop.

Paul delayed his return home by passing over the church to make a sacrifice. On his business trips, he had met a few women and bedded them all without any slight conscience. He had paid two prostitutes a lot of money for more pleasure and had vowed himself that he was going to offer a guilt sacrifice the instant he returned. Homeless boys in Gweru were easy to find because they often lingered around the church where they were offered free food. Most of them had lost their parents whilst some had run away from home in search of better living conditions.

He selected one and, when no one was looking, he took him inside the church, then down to the basement where he had had a secret altar built. With the sharp knife that had taken the souls of many innocent boys, he imitated Abraham's well-known sacrifice ritual.

The only difference in this act was that no sudden voice from God came and stopped him, no animal suddenly appeared to take the boy's place and the boys did really die.

Afterwards, Paul took care of the body as he had done with the others and went to the real altar, bowed down and prayed. He was disturbed minutes later when one of the church's workers informed him that there was an urgent phone call for him at his office.

Annoyed, Paul picked up the receiver. It was his mother and his anger rose.

'What do you want, mother? I haven't even spent twenty-four hours back in the country and you are all over me already.'

Diana was very direct when she told him the news. She hung up without giving him the opportunity of saying anything. Paul was immensely shocked. *Hadn't he just made a sacrifice?* It was very confusing, but it didn't change anything. Mollie had been killed in a car accident.

Mollie's body was flown to England and Paul was the one who personally broke the bad news to her parents. The parents said nothing. It was as if their daughter had been lost to them since the day she had left without saying goodbye. However, Mollie's brother and sisters were deeply hurt and felt offended. Paul was lucky to avoid being killed by one of the brothers who was ex-military. His sons were welcomed by their relatives and that was the only soother Paul could offer the Grants.

Paul spent a whole month in Wycombe trying to make peace with his in-laws. It was a lost battle and the reason he stayed longer was because the Grants wanted to see Mollie's children. At one point, he thought it was wise to leave them behind with their uncles and aunts, but Mollie's parents refused. They expected him to take full responsibility of his children. When the children recovered from a brief seasonal change illness, Paul returned to Zimbabwe craving for a sacrifice. He knew that Mollie's parents were never going to forgive him. He couldn't force them to forgive him, but he could at least ask for forgiveness by offering the heavens fresh innocent blood.

Paul returned home to find that his mother had been very busy. She had declined the offer of being at Mollie's funeral, wisely knowing that Mollie's parents weren't going to welcome her like they would have years ago when their children had married. Diana had no desire to meet them anyway. She had had diverse views on life that had collided with Mollie, but Diana had never hated her daughter-in-law. They hadn't gotten along well, that was true, but Mollie's presence had been a comfort.

With Mollie gone, Diana had made sure she salvaged the priceless opportunity of Paul's temporary absence to make herself part of the WT organization filling up the place Mollie had left. Mollie's sudden death seemed to attract more women to join WT. Diana used this as her major weapon to become an executive part of the company. Luckily, Ruvimbo liked her approach and helped her get the position as swiftly as she wanted it.

Paul returned to be met by these changes. After a torrid month with his in-laws, he barely had the strength to be surprised or go against his mother. The following day after his return, he left for Gweru and Diana suddenly remembered what she saw when she had visited the place. She felt herself tremble. Paul returned three days later with his eyes open. He noticed the remarkable change in WT and devised a profitable idea that his mother was ready to approve much to his surprise.

'I think it is a good idea,' Diana said, going over a daily paper. As the new co-owner of WT, her position required a firm update on the going-ons in the country.

'I thought you hated black women,' Paul pointed out.

Diana grunted. 'Our CEO is a black woman,' she said.

'You sure have changed over the month, what happened to you?'

'I discovered that my only child is more than what I had ever imagined,' Diana replied mysteriously.

Paul gazed at his mother and wondered what she was talking about. Used to her sarcasm, he thought nothing of it in the end.

'Have you seen Ruvimbo yet, to tell her about your new idea?' Diana continued after his silence.

'I'll do it in person, tomorrow,' Paul said. 'You really have transformed the company.'

'It was my unique way of mourning your wife, son,' Diana said calmly.

The rest of the week was spent recruiting new members for WT and Diana was pleased to see that Ruvimbo was neither enthusiastic nor negative against the idea. She was simply professional. Diana spent most of her thoughts on the business. She was trying so hard not to think about Paul and her discoveries. The number of adversaries increased daily as she ran WT. Diana had fired quite a number of Executives and the majority of Heaven's Ministry didn't like her at all for this. She used Ruvimbo whenever she wanted something from the church, especially favours that would enrich WT.

Diana met Ruvimbo's sister and invited her for lunch. Paul wasn't comfortable with the arrangement because every time he laid his eyes on Ruvimbo, his heart beat furiously. Ruvimbo was single and free to play with, but he didn't know why he couldn't approach her as he had endlessly done with all the other beautiful women he had met. He had slept with doctors, actors, singers, business tycoons and even lawyers, but all these ladies didn't possess something Ruvimbo had. The big problem was that he didn't have any idea what that *something* was.

The lunch that Sunday was exciting for Diana though it was abruptly interrupted by her visitor. She took the private detective she had hired to find out about her discoveries in Gweru to her isolated library. The man was often used by WT to do background checks on potential future members and business associates. It was one of Diana's innovative upgrades to the company.

Lancelot Maponga was a twenty-seven year old African man who had been a police officer for seven years before he changed his line of work. He had many connections and one of them had gotten him the job at WT. He missed nothing and as he stood in front of Diana Westwood, he sadly wished he had.

Diana had tasked him to Gweru to find out what Paul was doing every time he went there. Lancelot had thought she was just prying in her son's affairs, thinking that he was seeing someone without her knowledge. Diana hadn't given Lancelot a heads up on what he could possibly find. She had wanted to be sure before she assumed anything.

It took Lancelot two weeks to find what he was paid for and it had scared every brave bone in him. He didn't want to believe it at first, but the evidence was substantial to overlook. Paul Westwood was one sick man – that was for sure.

'Is your son around?' Lancelot asked his boss.

'Yes, let me check the halls before you say anything,' Diana said leaving the room. She returned in a few seconds. 'What did you find?' She asked after closing the door behind her.

'Did you know about this?' Lancelot asked pale.

'Know what, Mr Maponga?'

Lancelot produced a huge file from the briefcase he carried around with him for business. He opened the file and presented pictures from it.

'I had to develop these myself,' he explained. 'Here are pictures and sketches of twenty boys – missing boys – some of them homeless. These are pictures of those twenty boys courtesy of the mortuary. These are from the secret basement under the Headquarters of Heaven's Ministry. I am sure if you piece it all up with the blood stained clothes you saw in Gweru, you will know.'

Diana's huge frame fell into a sofa. She sweated profusely and Lancelot offered her his handkerchief and some nearby room glass of water.

'I wasn't sure at first but, but, Good Lord!' she breathed heavily.

'He is very lucky the police haven't figured it out yet. They can't link anything,' Lancelot said.

'Are you going to report him?' Diana asked, her courage and strength returning.

Lancelot shook his head. 'That's not up to me. I did what you asked me to and whatever you do with the information I discovered is your business, not mine,' he said professionally. The idea of a deranged wealthy white man killing black children sickened him, but he didn't want to be caught in it. There was no telling what would happen if he got involved.

'Thank you, Lancelot,' Diana said shocking Lancelot who was used to being formally addressed. 'I'll take care of it, personally. You'll receive your payment via your account with WT.'

'Thank you, ma'am.' Lancelot bowed slightly and left Diana to think about something he was no longer concerned with.

Chapter 11

The official story was that his cousin died of cancer, liver cancer that was ignored until it had reached an untreatable state. Paul knew the original story. Frank had died of AIDS. Paul went to a private clinic and was tested for the disease. The wait for the results was torture. He had been very careful with whomever he had slept with. Protection was part of the act. He often had intercourse with sexy African women and he didn't want to get any of them pregnant to cause what would become a disastrous scandal. The community saw him as a role model, a purely clean citizen who was good to the people and made Earth a better place to stay. This was one of the things that kept his company thriving and receiving local credits. His social identity was golden.

The results came out HIV negative and he was relieved. He chose to celebrate with another sacrifice and immediately left for Gweru. His latest sacrifice was a seven-year-old homeless black boy who liked to sniff glue and daydream of becoming rich. Paul sacrificed the boy knowing that he was doing both the boy and the community a favour.

He returned to Harare to be met by a new proposal. His mother wanted solely to own Women of Tomorrow. She offered to give him her shares in the Westwood Company in return. It was an offer Paul found himself extremely drawn to. His father had left Diana quite a lot of shares that made her one of the majority shareholders next to him.

Diana got what she wanted and since it was Ruvimbo's idea

all along, she gave her an extra 15%, topping up what Ruvimbo had personally bought. Her CEO was a very committed woman who deserved nothing, but praise, Diana thought. It was a month before Christmas and Diana was happy to get her present early that year. She became the owner of WT.

Nothing much changed at WT. Heaven's Ministry still anchored in various projects. The members increased weekly and the policies Diana had implemented remained the same. Paul saw less of his mother and felt like a prisoner being released from prison after a long sentence. He utilized his time well by taking some interest in his sons. They were growing up as he had – being loners. He had hired a good nanny who kept them in good shape. The boys saw their father like a stranger who popped up at intervals. He was a rich man who had the look of nothing, but money. They missed their grandmother more than they missed their mother.

Sixty plus years had passed since Diana had learned to walk. No matter how huge she had grown, she was always able to carry herself without difficulty. The first signs of the cancer came when she was attending a WT and Heaven's Ministry extraordinary meeting. She had felt very woozy on her bearings.

The family doctor had given her the bad news and Diana had known that her days were now numbered. She was going to have to leave her shares to someone. The only person she could think of was Ruvimbo. It wasn't something she liked to think about, but it was an unavoidable anomaly. She couldn't imagine what would happen if WT was thrust back into the hands of her son.

Although Diana wanted to keep her condition secret, her doctor was compelled to tell Paul. Paul didn't actually believe him because his mother had never seemed weak in his entire life. One of his troubling concerns though was the way the boys acted when Diana wasn't around. He wondered what it would be like the day when their grandma would be no more. The more time he spent with them, the more it saddened him. Part of him wanted his sons to grow up to become nothing like him.

Paul tried to take his mind away from these problems by

enjoying his electrifying affair with Ruvimbo. He couldn't actually remember how it had started, but he didn't care. Every fantasy he had ever had about her was slowly coming to life and he was by far amazed. Ruvimbo was a sweet maniac in bed. She satisfied all his wildest desires on the first days and now, by withholding sex from him, only made his head and heart want to explode.

They had slept together a total of three times before Ruvimbo started to avoid the act. At first, Paul was very careful with Frank in mind. It was an automatic instinct that he protected himself with rubbers every time he slept with her. He had no doubt that Ruvimbo was HIV negative for she didn't look like the type that slept around. Her image was so clean, the thought of her possibly having the virus was absolutely impossible to create. As time passed, Paul wasn't satisfied. He stopped using rubbers and enjoyed every moment of it. It was much better and real than before. He slowly fell in love with Ruvimbo no matter how hard he tried to deny his emotions from getting to his head. He visited Gweru and made his latest sacrifice

The sacrifice was a bit complicated because all of a sudden he didn't feel in control. He almost blew it when he was seen entering the church with a ten year old street urchin.

Many of his employees stared, but later thought nothing of it. Their leader was famed as a very generous man so they thought the boy couldn't be any luckier.

In the locked basement of Heaven's Ministry, Paul skilfully knocked the child out with commissioned medical anaesthetic. He said his prayers and chanted in soft song for a while. The first strike with the knife was miss-targeted. It pierced the child's lung rather than the intended heart. Plural cavity fluid oozed out and Paul clumsily tried to stop it. For the first time, he panicked and stabbed the child many times than necessary. Blood sprayed all over his clothes and he knelt defeated to the floor, ashamed of his first unclean sacrifice. He knew that his sacrifice wouldn't be accepted, so he cleaned up the mess and himself before taking a little altar wine to calm his nerves.

When the employees of the church, the few that worked till

ten P.M., saw Paul bring back another younger boy, they started to wonder what was going on. The talkative residential pastor exaggerated that Paul was venturing on a new *clean the streets and save the children* project. He bragged on about how he was going to build a big children's home and possibly imitate Jairos Jiri in the process. The curiosities were wiped out and Paul finally succeeded in a clean sacrifice.

Paul met Ruvimbo more every day. She seemed distant at times, especially when Diana was brought into the conversation.

'She doesn't look well, Paul,' Ruvimbo said as they had dinner at a hotel.

Paul shrugged. 'I know, but she refuses my help whenever I offer it,' he defended himself.

Ruvimbo didn't know why she was still seeing him for she had succeeded with her vendetta. Paul's sons were the only Westwoods left and she didn't know how she was going to finish it off. 'And you let her?'

'My mother is a strong-willed lady. Accepting help from anyone is like accepting to drink poison to her,' Paul replied.

He didn't want to argue with this wonderfully made woman. He didn't want to talk about his mother at all. Lately, Diana was very mysterious with him that he was getting very curious about what she knew.

'You could say that again,' Ruvimbo giggled nervously.

Paul noticed the oddity and focused his attention on her more. 'You on the other hand look troubled. What is it, love?' he asked sweetly.

Ruvimbo shook her head. 'Nothing, just my sister getting married.'

Paul was a bit taken back. 'Tendai, you mean Tendai?'

'Which other sister do I have, Paul, seriously?' Ruvimbo answered rather impatiently. Tendai's sudden arrangement made her very edgy.

'Oh,' Paul sighed. 'Fancy her getting married before you – it's very interesting.'

'What's so interesting about it?'

Paul grimaced. 'That you are still single, love.'

Ruvimbo frowned at him, but said nothing. Deep down, she felt her hatred for the Westwoods' family well up like an aquifer. *Your race and family are the reason I am never going to get married or have a chance to a happy life,* she thought heatedly.

Her date looked sideways thinking of other things, possible reasons why Ruvimbo was still single. Paul had the belief that Ruvimbo's social identity played a big role in it. She was intimidatingly successful than the majority of the men in the country. *Who would want a wife who was above them in society?*

Paul was however puzzled from these few views of his and what they showed. Ruvimbo's status was one thing, her appearance was definitely another. Her unique beauty was something even a man of a lower status would be hypnotized by to risk life itself. She was one of those rare finds wise men wouldn't dare waste a first time opportunity of just seeing her exist and letting her go untried.

Marrying Ruvimbo seemed to be the best thing to do for Paul, but he was so afraid she would turn him down or worse, discover his secrets. Diana on the other hand would never let him marry an African lady no matter who she was.

In the end, he thought that whomever Ruvimbo ended up with was going to be a very lucky gentleman.

Diana fought a mental battle with herself as she tried to figure out the best way to break the news. Ruvimbo was spending the weekend in Guruve executing some kind of Shona ritual.

Cancer was eating her away slowly, but that didn't deprive her the energy to plan for the future she wasn't going to live. Her mind was made up. Diana wanted Ruvimbo to own WT after her death. She wondered how Ruvimbo was going to react. When she had told the attractive lady that she had cancer, Diana had seen Ruvimbo cringe with emotion.

Knowing very well that Paul was now seeing her CEO on terms other than business, she was disturbed. There were dark corners Ruvimbo wasn't ever supposed to see. Diana was afraid

Paul's secrets were psychologically going to impale the sweet lady. It wasn't a conscience Diana wanted to die guilty of.

The issue was hard enough with her son being a very cunning handsome man. Diana couldn't see any way she could save Ruvimbo, but she didn't stop looking.

Her doctor had given her not more than a year to live. Diana knew that it was enough time to do what she needed to do. She had *everyone* in mind. Then, did she see how she had squandered a priceless opportunity of living a good memorable life. Her life seemed wasted and although she knew that there was no second chance, she was determined to make her last days more meaningful than the rest of her prior life.

Like almost everyone on Earth who had a past, she had secrets. There was one big secret she had kept for so long it seemed to have faded to nothing. She knew that it was time to make amends if she was to have a peaceful last breath when the day finally came. Her weekend was spent on the phone making international calls to her younger sister. Her mind was however on the future of WT. Diana was very worried that Ruvimbo would remain and head WT then later succumb to Paul's plans and marry him. Such an activity had dire consequences on the future of WT.

Once an independent women's organization, WT could possibly fall back into the hands of Paul Westwood. Diana was going to make sure such a scenario wouldn't be possible.

Paul returned from Ruvimbo's place anxious. He had found her house deserted like the day before and left her another note. He had thought she would have been home by three in the afternoon, but that wasn't to be. He started to panic a little, scared that something might have suddenly happened to her. She had become something like a drug to him similar to his sacrifice acts.

Was she still in Guruve? Had she met someone along the way? Was she alive? The questions taunted him on his drive back home that Sunday.

When he entered the house, he felt that something was out of place. He looked around and saw nobody, not even an employee of the house. As he was about to climb the stairs, a boy suddenly appeared on top of it. The boy's eyes were as white as his hair. His clothes were a black cassock that didn't show his hands or feet.

Paul stood there shocked. He shook his head and closed his eyes. The boy was gone. Frozen like a statue, Paul's eyes stared at the spot the boy had been. A sudden shuffling sound from the nearby sitting room brought him back to reality. Afraid of climbing the stairs anymore, he briskly made his way to the sitting room, wishing by all heart that he wasn't going to come face to face with another black boy with white hair.

The lady stood with her back to him. Her blond hair that fell a few inches below her shoulders instantly enchanted Paul. Her clothes looked so foreign Paul thought she was another hallucination. He cleared his throat and she turned slowly.

Ray's from the afternoon's sunlight reflected on her blond hair with her movements. For a moment, Paul thought he was seeing an Angel for the lady looked like nothing he had ever seen. She was definitely the most beautiful white lady he had come across in his entire life. Her skin was so white Paul thought his mind was playing tricks with him.

The young lady smiled at him and walked over raising a greeting hand at him. Paul moved a few steps back unsure of himself.

'I am sorry to jump on you like this, Mr Westwood, your gardener let me in,' the voice was strongly drenched in a British accent. 'This is my first visit to Zimbabwe.'

Paul was silent for a while. He looked around the room for any slight indication that this wasn't real. He didn't find it. 'I, I… what did you say?' he fumbled.

'It's my first time to be in Zimbabwe, although it was easy to find this place. Your house is very beautiful,' the young lady said. The warm pleasant smile she wore on her face didn't change.

'I am sorry, but do I know you?'

The lady rolled her eyes. 'I'm not sure, my name is Mary D. Wilson,' she said with confidence. 'I live in Portsmouth and arrived last night.'

Paul didn't know how to respond and ended up nodding. He

didn't have any idea what was going on or what the possibilities were.

'Diana asked me to come and see her,' the lady continued.

Paul raised his eyebrows. 'From all the way, I mean from Portsmouth?'

'Yes.'

Paul shook his head. This was very odd. He had no idea his mother had any friends left in England, what more a beautiful young lady. Perhaps she was going to be WT's new recruit. *However, why would a young lady of such qualities want to leave England to come to Africa?*

'I've only just arrived, I am sorry I don't know if she is around,' Paul said. 'Do you know her that well?'

The young lady grinned. 'I don't know. It's some long story.'

Paul's charm returned in full force. He sat down smiling and gestured to a nearby sofa. 'I have all the time in the world.'

'Thank you,' the lady said accepting the offer to sit.

'So how do you know Diana?' Paul began.

The young lady wasn't sure how she was supposed to say it so she sat back and just said it. 'From what I discovered only days ago, Diana is my biological mother. My full name is Mary Diana Wilson.'

The door to the sitting room suddenly swung open and Diana entered not knowing what was waiting for her. The two occupants turned to look at her and – from their blue eyes – she knew she had a lot of unexpected events to conclude her Sunday.

Chapter 12

The year began in a way nobody had ever anticipated. A lot had happened during the month of December. Some had thought the following months were going to be full of fireworks.

Tendai married Kudakwashe on the 23rd of December. It was a day that was going to be remembered for its unexpected events rather than the occasion itself. Many of the things that were expected to happen hadn't and those, which hadn't been supposed to occur, had hosted the event. Despite everything that had happened, it had been a great day.

On the 7th of January 2003, Kudakwashe greeted his brother-in-law and led him into their new house – a gift from his parents. Tendai dashed over to receive Bernard and his wife in warming gestures. Kudakwashe could see that his spouse was very excited about the get-together.

The two couples sat over dinner and discussed the country's current affairs. Kuda discovered that Bernard possessed the Dombokas' gift of intelligence during their talk. He was a very amiable person and Kuda couldn't help wondering a lot about the past and its consequential future.

As the two ladies did the dishes, the men sat over a bottle of wine watching a soccer match. Small talk emerged here and there. The ladies later joined them and the match was forgotten. It was about nine o'clock when Bernard asked the question of the day.

'How is your sister, Tendai?'

Tendai didn't look surprised. She had somehow thought of the moment all evening. 'I haven't seen or heard from her since the wedding,' she told him.

'I'm sorry I made things bad between you two,' Bernard said sadly. He felt guilty for the reason Tendai and Ruvimbo had had a fall-out.

'I don't think *Amaiguru* is willing to cooperate ever,' Kuda said sipping a little of his wine. 'I've spent the last few weeks talking to her, begging her to compromise.'

Bernard looked at him surprised. 'She actually speaks to you about such matters?'

'Ruvimbo is a good person. She gives me a chance to say what I want to say,' Kuda said. 'However, I can't say the same about you two.'

The room was silent for some time as they were all stolen away by different thoughts. Thirty minutes later, the new couple saw them out. They wished them a safe drive and promised another similar evening.

Paul had a hard time adjusting to the changes. He had spent a month trying to come to terms with the idea of Diana having conceived a child out of marriage. The fact that his mother had seen other men whilst she was supposed to be taking care of his ill grandmother back then didn't surprise him as much as her having a daughter and having had kept it a secret for so long.

There was no doubt that Mary was Diana's child. They both possessed the same eyes and mouth, although Diana's features were now weathered by age. The variance in character and attitude was however stunning. Mary was everything Paul had ever wished for as a sibling. She was very attractive, smart, kind and extremely friendly. Her near perfectness made Paul aware of everything he had done and how upturned it was.

Marry spent most of her time with her mother. She was returning to England early February to prepare for university where she was an Associate Professor of Haematology. Her time in Zimbabwe was like a summer break to her, not to mention that she was engaged and to be married that June. Paul avoided spending time with his little sister afraid that the flawless image she saw of him would be tainted if she looked closer.

'I never thought I'd see the day you'd be very uneasy in front of a lady,' Diana said one day when they were alone. Mary had visited Ruvimbo whom she had grown comely fond of from the very first day they had met.

'What are you assuming, mother?' Paul asked, not taking his eyes from the daily newspaper he was browsing.

'She makes you nervous, doesn't she?'

Paul shrugged and finally looked at her. The cancer was really changing her just as Mary's sudden appearance had changed her attitude.

'Twenty-eight years, mother, twenty-eight bloody years and you never thought it was actually nice to at least warn me that somewhere out there I...' he didn't finish.

'It was none of your business – why would I have told you?'

'Why now then? Why reach out to make her know you now, have her come all this way to see you?' Paul was appalled. 'I can't even believe that she came or that your sister actually told her who her real mother was, especially with her getting married so soon. Only if she knew the person you are.'

Diana frowned. 'People tend to do certain things they wouldn't when they face certain death. I always had that option to have your aunt tell her the truth – only that I didn't know it would be so soon. I'm dying – I needed her to know. Her wanting to see me and coming all this way was her choice.'

'Maybe when father was still alive, I'd understand the reservation to tell me, but I don't see any reason why, after all these years, you had me live with the belief that I was an only child – no matter the circumstances.'

'Would it have changed anything if you knew?' Diana asked.

It was pretty much a silly question because she knew that it could have made a whole lot of difference. It could have *saved* Paul.

Paul shook his head frowning. He hadn't made a sacrifice since the day his sister had arrived and since he started having hallucinations of young boys wearing small cassocks. He had also started having nightmares about his ex-wife blaming him for her accident.

It had worsened when Ruvimbo terminated their affair. She didn't want to entertain him in any way anymore. Paul sensed that something was very wrong, but he couldn't get Ruvimbo to tell him what it was. He was so pre-occupied with Mary and the day-nightmares to have the strength to fight for Ruvimbo's attention. WT had grown more efficient despite Diana's input decreasing weekly. Diana was spending more time at home just as Ruvimbo spent hers at work.

'How is your mistress?' Diana teased him.

Paul pretended to ignore her, but knew it wasn't a good idea. 'I have no mistress.'

'I guess so,' Diana said knowingly.

She was very happy Ruvimbo was no longer seeing his son. It was one of the few good things that came with the new year. Paul didn't like to be reminded of Ruvimbo. He missed her very much and the fact that he had come to care so much about her had made him respect her wishes. He kept his distance from her and hoped endlessly that she would reconsider.

The main door suddenly opened and closed with a huff. Paul felt her return before she even presented herself. Mary walked into the room they were sitting and went over to greet her mother with a kiss. Paul knew she was heading for him next and braced himself for the gesture.

'I hope you weren't talking about me,' Mary smiled at them sitting beside Diana.

Paul stared uneasily at his mother holding his breath. He hoped Diana wasn't going to be her old self and say something unorthodox.

'No, dear – how was your tour at Women of Tomorrow?' Diana returned the stare.

'Smashing! So different from spending a day in the labs teaching horny young mates,' Mary said excitedly. 'Ms Domboka is breathtakingly good-looking, not to mention her intellect and commitment.'

Diana watched Paul shift uneasily. She was certain he was going to leave the room any second from now. 'Those are points one would be very foolish to argue against,' she simply said

'I can't seem to get her accent out of my head. She sounds almost like me,' Mary noted her attention on her mother.

Paul folded his paper and flattened his tie. 'Excuse me, ladies, I got a meeting to get ready for,' he excused himself and left the room.

Mary stared after him confused. 'Was it something I said?' she asked Diana.

'No, dear, nothing you said at all.' Diana smiled reassuringly at her.

It was a sad thought that Paul was never going to let go of his feelings for Ruvimbo. It was also a blessing in disguise that those feelings had somehow some control over themselves

Having that unfortunate occurrence was something Ruvimbo hadn't thought about. Getting pregnant with a Westwood child was beyond bearable. For the first two months, she really tried hard to ignore her condition. She did a good job hiding it, but only a few wise older women at WT very much distinguished Ruvimbo and her former self. They all wondered who the father of the child was. Knowing that rumours had a higher percentage of being tainted and exaggerated, they said nothing in fear of what the news would do to the organization.

After terminating her affair with Paul, Ruvimbo had kept to herself – especially after the wedding. What Tendai had done to her was unforgivable. She had been shocked to discover that her little sister had invited their self-disowned brother to the wedding without even warning her. Similarly disturbed by her sudden pregnancy, Ruvimbo hadn't even at least attended the ceremony. It was now a month and a few days since she had last seen Tendai.

Kuda had paid her frequent visits, all centred on one issue. He had begged her to reconsider. Ruvimbo was touched by his persistent efforts and was pleased that Tendai had married him. He was one of the rare few good men in the world.

Ruvimbo was also very angry with Uncle Francis. He had known that Bernard was going to be at the wedding and although he wasn't comfortable with it, he had granted Tendai her wish. The Dombokas knew how Ruvimbo would react if she found out before the wedding, so they had gambled with nature and left it to the day. Ruvimbo knew that Uncle Francis wouldn't blame her for her actions. It was perhaps one of the reasons he hadn't approached her yet.

The intercommunication buzzer to her office linked from her secretary's office jerked her from her thoughts. Ruvimbo depressed a button and waited.

'Dr Chuma to see you, ma'am,' the secretary said.

'Is it a Mr or Mrs?'

'It's a Mrs, ma'am,' the secretary replied.

Ruvimbo gasped. 'I'm in an important meeting. Tell her I'll see her later.'

Ten seconds passed and the door to her office was forced open. Tendai came in fuming. She had a fierce look of determination Ruvimbo hadn't seen on her before.

'What the hell?'

Tendai went to stand in front of her desk in akimbo. 'This is your meeting?' she asked angrily.

'How dare you budge into my office like that?' Ruvimbo was on her feet in seconds. 'Leave, now!'

'Don't dare speak to me like that!' Tendai responded equally. 'I can't tolerate this nonsense anymore. Not from you, I won't.'

The two women stared heatedly at each other for not less than a minute.

'I told you to get out!' Ruvimbo emphasized her point with a frown.

Tendai folded her arms. 'I'm not going anywhere until we talk.'

Ruvimbo grasped her keys from the desk and rounded from her seat towards the door. 'Then enjoy your stay. I'll leave instead.' With that, she left the room slamming the door behind her

Tendai was stunned to make any move for a while. She ended up sinking into a chair, defeated. All her hopes faded away like mist in the wind.

Ruvimbo drove to a piece of undeveloped land at the fringes of the city. She found a deserted site where she parked her car and got out. She started walking toward no apparent destination. Hot tears welled up in her eyes and she felt her heart shrink. *Why was her life so complex?* Her vendetta quest was near completion and now she was pregnant. Ruvimbo knew that her days were numbered just as Diana's were. She knew that she was going to catalyse her death one day when the virus started to affect her. With a child in the picture, everything had changed. All the strength she had had stored up seemed to have disappeared.

Tendai was very determined to solve the issue that day that she passed by Ruvimbo's house around five in the evening. Nobody was at home, which wasn't at all odd. Disappointed, Tendai left the house heading for her uncle's place. Uncle Francis was relaxing on a sofa, preparing for a shift he was supposed to be taking that night.

'How do you do it?' Tendai asked. 'You are almost dozing off and yet you'll have like a dozen of patients to attend to today. I can never look so calm.'

Uncle Francis laughed without opening his eyes. 'That must be why you chose to become a vet instead of the real thing.'

'At least humans don't bite, dogs surely do and what could be more real.'

Uncle Francis continued laughing. 'A bit tense, are we, today? Your Aunt told me that you were planning to see your sister today. Did you?'

'I did see her and I really don't know what to say,' Tendai smiled at her aunt as she joined the two. 'Good evening, Aunt.'

'Evening, Tendai,' Mrs Domboka went over to sit next to her. 'How did it go with Ruvimbo?'

'If I had known she was going to be like this, I'd have never invited Bernard to the wedding. She wants absolutely nothing to do with me and believe when I say *nothing!*'

'Give her some time – she will eventually come around,' Mrs Domboka said reassuringly.

Tendai wasn't the least convinced. 'I'd very much want it to be like that, but there is something about Ruvimbo nowadays. It's like she doesn't recognize me at all when she looks at me.'

Uncle Francis left the two women later that evening worried. He somehow felt like he had lost Ruvimbo at the price of acknowledging Bernard back into the family. It was a decision he wished he hadn't been compelled into for nothing in the world could matter more to him than his gorgeous successful niece. She was a rare jewel and he knew he had to make things right.

Chapter 13

The visit to the family doctor was mainly for his mother's check-up, but it had turned out differently in the wind. Paul had collapsed after hallucinating of yet another black boy wearing a cassock.

Mary had just left a month ago and Diana wasn't the same. Mary had left under Diana's strict orders for she had opted to stay a while longer. Mary had made them promise that they would make an effort to attend her wedding that June, which both mother and son had done so with poker faces. It was a miracle that Diana hadn't told her only daughter that she had cancer with only a few months or less to live. Paul was surprised, but didn't interfere. His sister's departure left him vulnerable and he had no idea why.

During her last days in Zimbabwe, Mary had made an incredible effort to bond with her brother. The effort had triumphed much to Diana's surprise. Mary was someone everyone automatically got endeared to and Paul's antagonistic and confused feelings had failed to be exceptions.

Diana took Paul's collapsing less serious assuming that it was the stress overclouding him. Her son was a cold-blooded psychopath, what could make him so stressed enough to faint?

The family doctor checked Paul's blood for anything unordinary when he tried to discover why he had collapsed. The answer came up really fast. He had no idea how he was going to break the news. When Diana's weekly check-up was over, the doctor asked Paul to return that evening for his own check-up. He assured him that everything was okay and Paul agreed to be there without asking any questions.

That afternoon, Ruvimbo saw her own doctor who told her that her pregnancy was progressing on well. The doctor asked her if she wanted to know the sex of the baby and after a moment of hesitation, Ruvimbo let him tell her. She left the hospital shocked.

Was it a bad omen or karma? She was carrying a boy, a Westwood *boy*.

Ruvimbo had dedicated her life to erasing the Westwoods' family by mainly eradicating the males who inherited the genes and blood of the generation. The fact that she was now carrying one in her womb was sickening. It was very ironic in a dozen ways.

Paul wasn't going to live long, which was an unavoidable truth. She had injected him with a large dose of *Istreblyat'* and – knowing that she had AIDS – there was a great chance Paul had it too. The only Westwoods who weren't affected were Paul's two boys.

She had been planning on how she was going to take care of them when she had discovered that she was going to conceive one of them. Confused as she was, Ruvimbo knew that she had to finish what she had started no matter what. This was the endgame. She knew she had to do it fast before she changed her mind.

Diana lay on her bed and knew that the day had finally arrived. She had planned well for it and she knew how to execute each step without fear.

'Ma'am, he is here. Should I see him in?' her nurse aid peeped into her room.

'Thank you, please send him in,' Diana said energetically for someone whose time was ticking away.

The *visitor* entered her room and was taken aback by how calm and fragile Diana looked. It was a moment he realized that all mortal beings had expiring dates. Diana smiled weakly at him and was a little bit saddened that he was possibly going to be the last man she was ever going to see. The two talked for thirty minutes before the visitor was forced to leave against his wishes.

The visitor left with his eyes moist. His heart was torn apart by what he had seen and that only motivated him to carry out his task.

Diana called for the nurse. 'Can I see my grandchildren, please?' she begged.

The boys were brought in for a long hour with their granny. They left the room cheerful, a sight that sadden the nurse

Diana took her album and started to flip it over, the nurse sitting by her bedside. There were pictures of her mother and father in black and white film. Then came pictures of her brothers and sisters, mainly the sister who looked after Mary and had married Mary's father. Her other siblings were all dead and she knew that her sister would be the only one left in a few minutes or hours.

She looked on to the pictures of her deceased husband and Paul. They were pictures filled with the sorrows of life. Next were the recent pictures of her daughter. Diana stared into those eyes and saw part of what she had been when she was young – so full of life and hope. She hoped Mary would one day understand. It was really better this way. Her last thoughts fell on Ruvimbo and WT. She smiled and closed her eyes *forever.*

The night watchman of Heaven's Ministry was stunned when he saw four black cars parked in front of the church. They had government plates. There was no mistaking their criteria. It was around seven o'clock in the evening and he was about to take over from his colleague.

Seeing police cars at a church wasn't a good sign at all. *What is going on?* He thought. He advanced closer to get a better view. Many of HM's employees were standing at the doors holding their mouths or chins. It was clear that whatever had happened had shocked all of them.

Three days had passed since the passing away of their leader's mother. Funeral arrangements had been their main priority for the past few hours. Rumours were that Paul was going to give his mother a flamboyant send away. His theme was said to be focused on celebrating Diana's life rather than her departure from the world. Those who didn't know were surprised to discover that Diana had had a daughter, meaning that their leader had a sister. All that was forgotten when the police arrived to come out of their cars heavily armed. They hadn't even interrogated anyone about anything, but had barged into the church full of purpose.

'What's going on?' the night watchmen asked his colleague.

His colleague shook his head. 'I don't know. They aren't saying anything and we are wise enough not to ask. They are CID, serious business.'

'But this is a church, don't they respect that?' the night watchman asked partly annoyed.

'Better not let them hear you say that.'

The people waited anxiously. Suddenly the doors to the main hall were pushed open. Two plain-clothes police detectives appeared with Paul in the middle. His hands were cuffed in front of him and he was furiously struggling to get free. Two others wearing black suits followed – a man and a woman.

'Get your damn hands off me!' Paul shouted.

'Let's not make a scene, Mr Westwood,' one of the detectives said firmly.

Paul forced himself to one side and looked back. He glared threateningly at someone. 'You set me up, you son of a bitch.'

'Mr Westwood, I didn't set you up. I was only following precise and clear orders,' the man replied uncharacteristically calm.

'Following orders from who, you *wart*? You bloody work for me,' Paul snarled as the detectives struggled to keep him still.

'From your mother, sir,' the man replied.

Paul shook furiously. 'How dare you – how dare you talk about her when you know that she is dead.'

'Everybody knows that Mrs Westwood is at peace now, Mr Westwood,' Lancelot said and watched the police officers force Paul into one of the cars.

The crowd watched shocked. Lancelot briefly sighed at last, satisfied. He had carried out Diana's last wish. He had *saved* Paul.

Ruvimbo agreed to meet Uncle Francis to discuss the issue about Tendai and Bernard at his office that day. She had a motive towards her long-term plan. Uncle Francis was very happy to see her.

'I thought I'd never see that beautiful face again,' Uncle Francis said. 'I'm glad you came – you have grown big since we last saw each other,' he said noting her pregnancy with a specialist's eye.

'It's the least I can do,' Ruvimbo said.

'I really appreciate you seeing me on short notice, especially when it's something you don't want.'

Ruvimbo smiled politely. 'Seeing you is something I don't have a problem with at all, Uncle. It is what we have to discuss when I see you that I don't favour.'

'I know, niece, even I don't want to talk about it, but I promised your sister I'd try my best.'

'So you have forgiven Bernard?'

Dr Domboka avoided her gaze. 'As much as I don't like it, I truly can't live the rest of my life ignoring his efforts to make up for his mistakes.'

'You aren't answering my question,' Ruvimbo said harshly.

'I'm forced to forgive him because it will only make things worse if I don't. Tendai isn't backing down on this one.'

Ruvimbo stood up and began to pace around the room. 'I don't believe you two. I surely don't.'

'I'm begging you to do the same, Ruvimbo,' Uncle Francis said. 'You got a great life ahead of you to worry yourself about what your brother did or didn't do. Let this pass, just acknowledge him and live your life without hatred or remorse eating your heart. It's not worth it.'

'You have no idea what I am now, Uncle. If only you knew,' Ruvimbo looked blank as she stared at an HIV poster on the walls.

Uncle Francis leaned on his desk to get a better look at her. He didn't understand her and seeing her produce tears ultimately stunned him. Ruvimbo never cried. She was a lady made of steel nerves.

Suddenly, the door to his office was opened. One of the junior intern doctors stopped short when he saw Dr Domboka with a visitor.

'Sorry, sir, I thought you were alone,' he apologized. His gaze lingered on Ruvimbo and he couldn't move for a few seconds.

Uncle Francis grinned as he saw the junior doctor undeniably mesmerized by his niece's appearance. 'It's okay. John, what is it?'

John shook his head and blinked. 'Er – patient C751's son wants to see you. He says he isn't going to leave the hospital until he personally thanks you.'

'I'll be with you in a moment,' Dr Domboka said smiling.

The junior doctor couldn't resist taking one last look at Ruvimbo. He left blushing.

Ruvimbo saw her priceless opportunity appear out of nowhere. 'Please go, I'll wait for you,' she said taking a seat.

'Are you sure?' Uncle Francis asked her.

'Please go,' Ruvimbo smiled reassuringly.

Hours later at home, Ruvimbo made sure everything was in place when she opened her briefcase and produced the medical instruments she had stolen from Uncle Francis's office. Ruvimbo stared at her diary and finally found the strength to write the names of Paul's two boys beneath their father's name. It was nearly over. Only one Westwood remained. Her mind strayed on Paul for a while. All the crimes Paul was charged with made her relive her dream. Rumours were spreading around like fire. What she had done was justified and there was no question about it. The only sad thought she had was about the two boys. They had suffered for the sins of their race and family. The room suddenly fell silent as she thought of her life and what had become of it. She took one of the medical instruments, opened her legs wide and without hesitation, killed the last male Westwood.

Final Part

Natural Windows

July 2003 – Harare

Chapter 14

The maximum prison's atmosphere stirred both grief and anxiety in her as the officer checked her credentials. Two prison guards stared at her and wondered what such a beautiful lady was doing at such a hellhole.

'Your inmate has been very disturbed for the past few days. Are you absolutely sure it's a good idea to see him now?' the officer asked her.

Tendai nodded. She wanted to know and since she had come this far, she knew that there was no going back. She had pulled a lot of strings to get this meeting approved. 'Yes, please.'

The officer saw the unrest in her eyes and sighed. He opened the gate for her and gave her a visitor's pass. He called out to one of the prison guards and assigned him as her escort.

A few minutes later, a fence divided the inmate and Tendai. The guard stood a distance away giving them privacy.

The inmate stared at Tendai and flinched. It was like he was seeing ghost. 'Ruvimbo?'

Tendai shook her head. 'It's me, Tendai,' she corrected him. She had grown to look very much like her sister in the past few months. The shock, stress and pregnancy had ironically aged her into a very appealing sight.

'Oh,' the inmate looked down.

'How have you been, Paul?' Tendai asked.

Paul looked up and saw that she was genuinely concerned. *How could she?* He thought. He was awaiting trial to face multiple life sentences in jail. Mr Grant and his associates had assured him that they would get him out soon, but he knew that whatever the case, he wasn't going to live long. Some deadly virus was swiftly eroding him off his days of living. It was a miracle he had survived for so long.

'You are the first visitor I have had,' Paul said, his eyes looked dreamy. The hallucinations hadn't stopped. They haunted him endlessly that he screamed sometimes. His isolated *cell* made it worse.

Tendai realized that her time was limited and she had no plans of ever returning to that place, so she started to do what she had come for. 'Why did you do it, Paul? Why?'

'I guess for the same reason you killed my children,' Paul giggled

The officer had been right. Paul wasn't in his right mind, she observed. He still thought she was Ruvimbo.

'I'm very sorry about that,' Tendai said, fighting her tears back.

'What did I do to you that was so bad?' Paul stared at her, his expression incredibly calm.

'That's why I am here, Paul. I want to know what I did and why I did it,' Tendai played along.

'We had great times, didn't we? I almost asked you to marry me.'

This was news to Tendai. *Had Ruvimbo known that Paul had been a killer all along? Was it the answer she was looking for?* 'Did I know you murdered all those boys?' she asked.

Paul laughed hysterically. 'Mother knew, you didn't,' he said.

Ruvimbo's death had caused a quake. Uncle Francis was so shocked he had retired from practicing medicine. It was one of his surgery's medical instruments that Ruvimbo had used to kill her unborn child.

She had bled to death at her home, something she had anticipated and allowed to happen. It was both murder and suicide at once. Before that, she had collected Paul's children from their private school acting as if she was doing Paul a favour in the eyes of the schools' staff as Paul was currently in police custody.

They had watched her leave with the kids with no questions. She was after all one of the most influential women in the country and rumoured to be Paul Westwood's mistress.

The boys had accepted poisoned plastic bottled refreshments from her and two hours after being dropped at the Westwoods' mansion with a sealed letter to their nanny, they had reacted to the poison and died within minutes. The letter had a single line, which read:

What your ancestors did to mine, I do unto all of you for Justice.

Bernard had understood then. He had remembered how his parents had been killed and how it had resultantly affected Ruvimbo. All these years she had lived with a *mission*. She had succeeded. He discovered everything she had done and made out the rest when he discovered how the Westwoods had died over the years and how his sister was connected. It was a painful truth that Ruvimbo had facilitated the death of more than twenty men, children as well. *Who knew how many more who had suffered as collateral damage, all by just playing to their weaknesses and lust?* It couldn't be called direct murder for there was really no proof of her being a serial killer, but there was no running away from how the Westwood boys had died. It was *cold murder* in all expressions of the nature.

Tendai knew that Bernard and her uncle had discovered possibilities of why Ruvimbo had done what she had done, but they weren't telling her. She also knew that no matter how hard she tried to persuade them to tell her, they were never going to. They were very scared of what the truth would do to her. She had ventured on her own path in search of the truth.

'Did you know I was pregnant with your child?' she asked.

Paul looked at her for a few seconds, and then seemed to snap out of it. 'You did well to hide it. Guess you discovered that I gave you AIDS so you killed my sons and our son and oops – yourself.'

Tendai was amazed by how much detail Paul knew whilst he was mentally switching on and off. *So Paul had infected Ruvimbo with AIDS,* she thought. That was motive.

Tendai left the prison satisfied. She thought that she had her answers. Ruvimbo had been an extremely successful young woman with a golden future ahead of her. Paul Westwood had seduced and infected her with a deadly incurable disease as well as impregnating her with a child who was going to be born with the disease. That was a reason enough to make someone snap and kill Paul's sons.

She saw her brother on her way home that day and told him about her find. Bernard agreed with her. He was saddened by the fact that what Tendai thought was the truth was far from it. Whatever the case, he knew that sometimes it was better knowing your own truth than the real truth. It was a necessary lie.

The tombstone looked immaculate. Such places made Mary shrink as she knew that one day she was going to die. Her hair fell over her face as she knelt down and placed her flowers on it. The letters inscribed on the tombstone were clear. *Some things in life never make sense,* she thought

Mary read Ruvimbo's name once more and closed her eyes. There lay the woman who had poisoned her nephews, the woman who had been the backbone of her inherited company, the woman who had been perfect in appearance and a mystery deep inside.

When they had first met, Mary was instantly attracted to Ruvimbo. She was her role model and the few weeks Mary had spent in Zimbabwe had made her appreciate Ruvimbo more and more.

Paul had called her to inform her of Diana's death. She had to travel to Zimbabwe with her then-mother now-aunt for Diana's funeral. When they had landed in Harare, they had been met by a tyranny of shocks.

She discovered that Diana had died of cancer and her brother had been arrested accused of killing more than fifteen boys. The allegations were so strong that Mary had found it logical not to ignore them. Around the same time of Paul's arrest, Ruvimbo had killed her nieces – and herself. In comparison to what Paul was said to have done, what Ruvimbo had done had been excused as a crime of passion and revenge for many people to overlook its seriousness. She had been forced into the spotlight during her mother's funeral, people she didn't know wanting or demanding answers from her. Without Diana, Paul, Mollie, the children and even Ruvimbo, she had automatically become the person everyone had their eyes on.

Following the advice of her aunt, they had quickly left the country after the funeral. Back in England – soon after – Diana's lawyer had contacted her to inform that she was the sole heir of Diana's assets, including part of Women of Tomorrow. A lot of things didn't make sense, and she still had a lot of questions. Her family in England had advised her to take care of that part of her life first before the wedding and she had done just that. The last few months had made her slowly understand what had happened, having to return to Zimbabwe yet again, consequentially having to postpone her wedding to September.

Now the owner of WT, she had asked Tendai to be her CEO. After a month of no success, she had finally managed to persuade Tendai to occupy the position, with an option to transfer her inherited shares for Tendai to own the company solely after Tendai was ready after her pregnancy's phase. There were rumours about what had happened to Ruvimbo at the organisation. They were quite a lot of them that in the end only a countable few knew the real story. Tendai's occupation of her sister's former position made the rumours fade away and WT expanded each week with Mary's youthful leadership and Tendai's status and wisdom.

As advised by her legal counsel, soon after inheriting the entire Westwood Company because of being the only close blood relative of a Westwood of legal claim – with no Westwood left – Mary had stripped Heaven's Ministry apart, its assets sold in an effort to erase its existence and Paul. The money from the sales was centred toward charity organisations that centred on the homeless, especially children, much more of a publicity incentive to help people heal from what Heaven's Ministry now stood for.

Many people asked about Paul and she told them that she didn't know anything. It was the truth. The only things she knew were little unproven facts. Paul's lawyer, who was his brother-in-law, said one thing, the police and media said another. It put her in a tricky position, especially out of nowhere having to discover whom her biological mother was to seeing her, returning to England only to return to discover she had inherited a fortune that was marred with controversy and all that in less than six months.

She knew that Paul was somehow psychologically disturbed. He had used religious delusions as incentives that enabled him to murder small boys. Diana had discovered about it and had made Lancelot set a trap for Paul. Paul had been caught red-handed by the authorities of the Law – Diana's last desire as Lancelot had told Mary.

She wished that she could have been introduced to her family younger and perhaps everything could have been very different.

Ruvimbo's story was a mystery of its own. Mary knew that in all her years to come, she was going to forget about the complicated past, heal and possibly live a happy future.